CORRECTED

CORЯECTED

AUTO|CORRECT: JUVENILE DETENTION

Robert L. Hawkins III

H

Hawkins Enterprise Group

Cover design by A'Lexa's Designs

First Edition: January 2021
ISBN: 978-0-9849477-3-7

The Hawkins Enterprise Group
hawkinsenterprisegroup@gmail.com

Printed in the United States of America

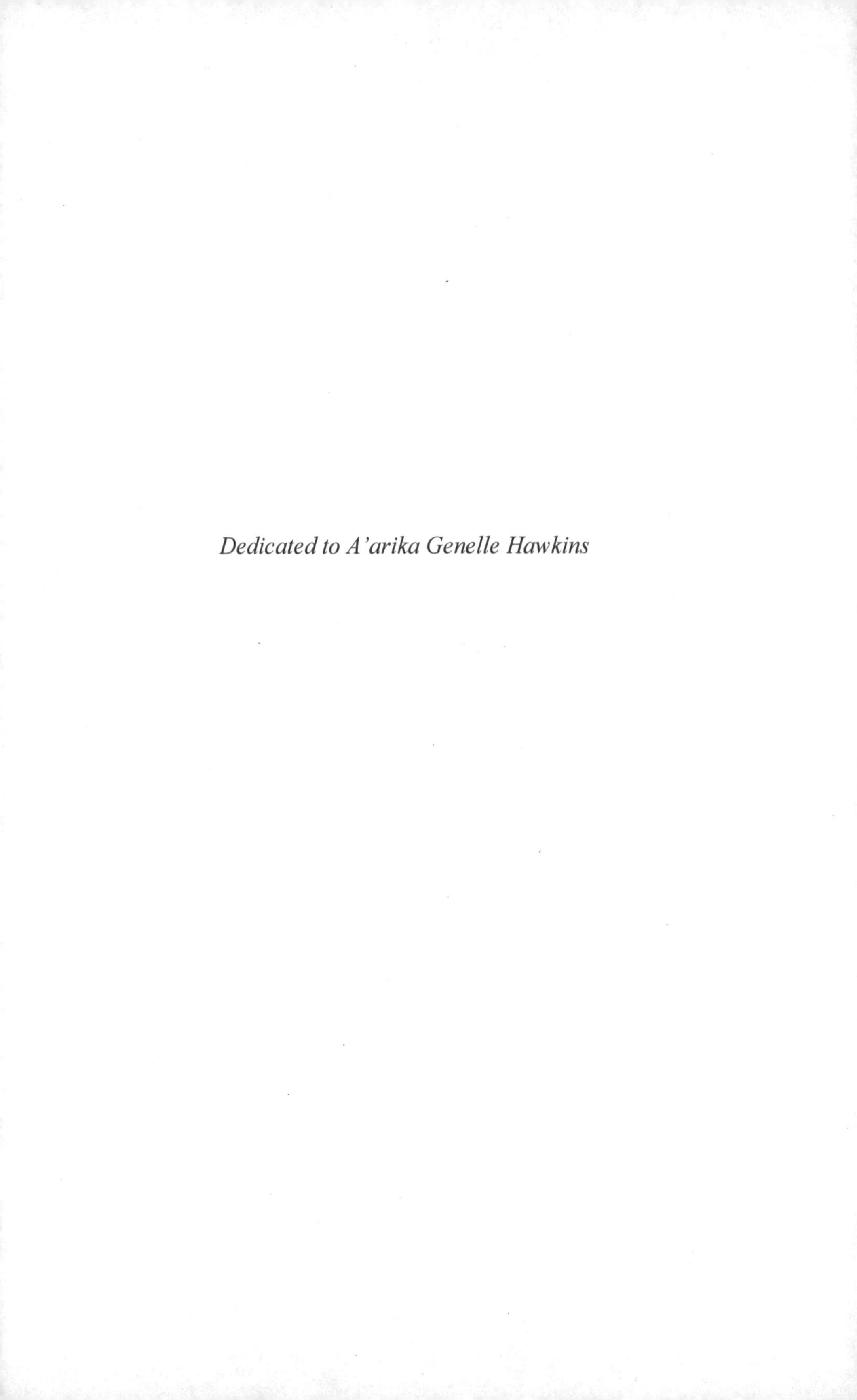

Dedicated to A'arika Genelle Hawkins

Part 1

Another Morning

"Good morning residents. Please wake up and open your eyes. Consequences for failure will begin in 5 minutes", the robotic voice stated calmly from the ceiling speakers. Shakeem sighed and opened his eyes knowing that today, even with the changes, would be just like all the others. He rolled over on his cot in his small room and sat upright, looking at the glowing blue camera-like orb mounted on the wall. Next to it was a button along with a small speaker. He made eye contact with the orb until the light turned green, and then rubbed his eyes. "Eye contact completed, Good morning resident 3022, J. SHAKEEM, you appear in good health". The voice was quieter this time, a localized prompt from the mother computer. The ceiling speakers were instructions for everyone. Shakeem rubbed his neck where the thin metallic collar met his skin, the collar where consequences would be administered if he were to step out of line. He stood up and walked to his tiny desk and swung out the stool that connected to the white wall. He looked at a picture of himself with his sister; two dark-skinned teenagers, smiling in the sun miles away from this concrete building. He gazed at two happy children, both of which were gone now. Shakeem waited by the large metal door directly in front of his cot, and after the speaker gave the second warning, "30 seconds until consequences. Please stand by your doors", he heard the inevitable screams. Two or three of the residents were not up on time and consequences were administered. The metal door swung open, and

Shakeem, along with 29 of his other neighbors stepped out onto the pod floor.

The floor of the pod had various luminescent lights that lit up into patterns, typically straight or curved lines that told each person where they were to be standing. A small light on the collar would activate, illuminating the front and back of the individual's shirt with a specific color. At the same instant that the color appeared on the shirt, a colored line would appear within the floor. The resident would look down, see their color, and move to the corresponding line. For morning-hygiene, residents were to follow the green line to the hygiene vendor, and then to the bathroom. Shakeem stood on the green line that had not fully lit up. If the line was not completely illuminated, no one was to move forward. To move would be a consequence, and consequences were never missed. He looked around the pod, a hexagonal shaped room with five rooms on each wall. He saw resident after resident step out onto the line, some immediately as he did, and some after a few seconds. He then saw the few residents who had been late. They rubbed their necks and twitched slightly. They were not use to consequences or the collars yet, but they would be soon. The speaker continued as the floor lines became brighter until they were fully illuminated. "Please follow the pathway to pick up your hygiene supply." All at once, the residents turned, and moved counter clockwise to stop briefly at a vending slot by the bathroom door. The hygiene vendor was a simpler machine. Two basic functions only, no human relation programming what so ever. It was more like a water fountain than anything else; a twist or a push, then a service. It was simple, and Shakeem preferred simple. This machine you could lie to. This machine you could hold something back from. The others, not so much.

When it was Shakeem's turn, he placed his finger print on the scanner and from a small collection bin came a box. The box contained his deodorant, a soap container, a toothbrush, toothpaste, and a hair brush. Shakeem picked up his transparent little box and moved along the green line, careful not to step off the line for too long. He entered the bathroom complex, as the green line led him, along with his other residents following the green line to his designated hygiene spot. There were only 6 hygiene spots, complete with everything one would need. The small enclosed space held a toilet, a shower head, a drain, a chute for dirty clothes a sink, and dry towels. One was to use all they needed within the allotted time frame, 10 minutes. The speakers on the ceiling were quick to remind everyone of the rules. "Please follow the green lines to your designated hygiene area. You will have ten minutes for hygiene once the water is activated. The countdown will start momentarily. Tardiness will have consequences". Shakeem stepped into his shower area, where there were no guide lines on the floor. Instead, there were black lines surrounding the hygiene area. Shakeem didn't need a reminder. He knew what would happen if he stepped out of the shower area before his time was up. He quickly took off his shirt and pants from the previous day, and stuffed them into a chute on the wall. He turned on the water, and waited 15 seconds for the water to heat up. He placed his toiletries on the sink, and applied tooth paste to his brush and sat on the toilet for a brief moment before wiping and stepping into the stream of water from the shower head. He brushed his teeth while in the shower, needlessly saving time. He finished showering with his soap, and rinsed his tooth brush. He placed everything back in his box, after using the deodorant sparingly. He stood by the wall, naked for a moment, and then used a towel to dry off. He sat on the toilet and looked behind him, to the other residents staring at him.

The next resident in line behind him was eager to start his shower, and so he mumbled,
"Move out the way so I can start".
Shakeem looked at him, and mumbled, "You're a new intake, aren't you?"
The resident looked around and said, "I don't care about consequences. Nigga, I run this shit".

Before Shakeem could consider being insulted the resident fell to the ground and began to tremble. His mouth locked in place as drool started to leak onto the bathroom floor. Other residents in other lines, waiting to shower looked away, and after a second, Shakeem did too. The resident on the floor gasped and clutched his neck, his body still writhing in pain until his body collapsed into a calm, still position. His chest heaved in and out, catching his breath, and finally he could speak again. The other residents continued their conversations, and showers as normal, and the resident on the ground stood up, stepped back onto the green line which was glowing. A small localized speaker, embedded into the collar of the resident stated, just barely enough for Shakeem to hear, "A 5 second consequence for aggressive, intimidating behavior and language was administered. Please be mindful of your interactions with other residents. Thank you!" The new intake looked at the floor.

Shakeem's time was up, and a new line appeared on the ground. His collar lit up an orange color to match the color of the guide line. As he passed the new intake resident, they exchanged glances, one that said, "I'm sorry", and another that said, "I know". There was a small whiff of urine in the air. Shakeem moved quickly along the orange line, meeting up with others who were also finished. This line took them first toward the hygiene collection slot, where a simple finger print scan and a slot for the hygiene box was revealed, and then back to their rooms where they were to get dressed and wait. Residents were free to move about as they wished in their room, they were also free to say what they'd like. While the rooms were not entirely sound proof, they were the only place of privacy the residents had until treatment time. Shakeem opened one of the many drawers that lined the wall of his room and took out a green t-shirt, and green sweat pants, both with the fancy curly white logo stating, "Paris Youth Correctional Facility". The logo would reflect the ever-changing colors of the collar, so he was clear on what line he was supposed to be on. He put them on, and now, accurately labeled, sat at his desk and looked at the door until the showers were complete.

A cheerful melody played from the ceiling speakers, and then a message. "Good Morning Residents. Today the schedule will be as follows: After morning hygiene there will be a dining period, then we will proceed to the education pavilion. From there we will have a small period of free time and then a second dining period. From there, there will be a period of reflection for those who are not scheduled to meet with treatment teams, and for those who are on the roster, they will go to the counseling pavilion. After this, we will have our physical training hour and the third dining period. Medications will be dispensed directly after this period. After this there will be time, for those who are eligible, to enjoy free-time on their available cluster. Any questions will be answered now."

After that, the small button on the side of the glowing green camera also lit up green. If there were questions, the resident was to push this button to activate the microphone. Shakeem couldn't think of anything to say, not any question that would be answered by the automated response system. In the past he had tried. He had asked exactly what time it was, or if it was raining outside. He would ask if he was doing well, or maybe if he could get out earlier. He asked why fools fall in love, or if the pope would be by to visit him today. He'd asked these questions, sometimes in seriousness, and sometimes in jest, but most of the time in regret. The box on the wall was mostly silent. Mostly.

It was time. Shakeem stood on the line outside his door, as the colors changed. He was to move away from the blue guide line and onto the purple ones closer to the center of the room. He stepped over quickly, knowing there was only a few seconds allotted for transitions. Any longer than this and there would be consequences. He looked around for the new intakes, and saw that they were following the rest of the residents fairly well so far. It wasn't always an easy process.

As they walked around the pod toward the pod main door clockwise, they passed the hygiene vendor and the hygiene room, both of which were dark and lifeless. The main pod door, with a large C printed on it, parted in the middle and each side slid into the wall. The residents left the living pod space and were entering the cluster floor. Pod C was located above the other pods, and thus there were stairs leading downward onto the large open area referred to as the cluster. The entrances to pods A, B, C, and D were placed on the walls of the cluster, and the center of the cluster was kept clear for free time or other events. Pod B was directly below pod C, and was considered underground, where pod A and D were on the same level of the cluster. Shakeem stepped out of the pod door and looked out over the cluster where lines of residents were formed in their various tracks and moving around the cluster in unison. Some of the new intakes were looking eagerly around, attempting to capture every detail in their head. The veterans barely looked ahead. Shakeem was somewhere in between. He knew why some of the residents were here, and he knew how dangerous they were, yet at this moment, they were docile, controlled; calm. He did note, however, that every now and then there would be a resident who purposefully stepped off their designated guide line, and clutched their neck briefly, and returned to their line. Small consequences for small deviations. Large consequences for larger deviations. Immobilization for violent behavior, and worse for the potential of mortal or lethal harm.

While on the cluster, and during transitions, there was to be no speaking. One only needed to follow the line which corresponded to the color of their collar at the moment. No questions needed to be asked, merely obedience. The schedules were staggered to fit everyone into the day, usually pod A would awaken first, eat and be returning as pod B was doing hygiene, and so on. Sometimes the schedule would be different and go in reverse order, sometimes the schedule would change in the middle of the day as needed. But as always, no questions were answered as none were necessary. The voice spoke, the lights changed, the residents moved.

As Shakeem walked around the cluster and to the cluster door, he noticed his color blinking, and slowly changing from purple to yellow. He looked down frantically to see where the yellow line was. Just to the right of him, the yellow line began to glow, and so, in a single step, he moved over. The resident in front of him did as well, and then the others. Within a few seconds everyone had moved from purple to yellow, and as the last person made his way to the yellow line, the large cluster door opened. They were on their way to the dining hall.

The residents, careful to stay in line and careful to remain silent in the halls, shuffled meticulously down the long hallway. The yellow line seemed to pulse beneath them, meaning that this was an active line, residents were moving along this pathway. As they moved down the 500-foot hallway, they noticed another lit up line become active. Some checked their colors to see if they were to switch lines, but this wasn't the case; their colors remained yellow. The dark brown line a few feet away from the yellow began to pulse and grow brighter, and residents passed by going the opposite direction.

New intakes were often forgetful of the rules despite the constant overhead warnings and the group action. Because of their un-rehabilitated state, they clearly lack the discipline, or the memory, of the consequences. As the brown-lined residents shuffled past, one of the new residents reached out to a yellow-lined resident.

"Hey Cody, Cody! When did you get in man, I miss…" the resident fell to the floor in writhing pain.

"Yo! Mack! Hey!...", the resident everyone assumed was Cody also fell to the floor, in pain. Both residents writhed as the lines changed from a pulsing yellow and brown light to fragmented ones. Dashes of light, rather than a continuous line formed, which meant for the other residents to stop movement. The veterans, and smarter intake residents stood there, quietly, and watched. The two residents on the ground were not fast learners. They screamed and yelled and asked for help. The other residents merely stared.

"Fuck all ya'll then!" yelled Cody, as he experienced another surge of pain in his body, gasped for air, and wriggled on the ground once again.

"Please…" gasped Mack, "please, no more", as he struggled to get onto his feet.

"No Talking In The Hallways Please", said the voice in the ceiling speakers. "Please comply to avoid consequences".

Mack stood up straight, after a few moments, and stood in his line quietly. Cody continued to resist, receiving shocks every three seconds while he cursed and muttered. The other residents in the line stood still and quiet, some of them with tears in their eyes as they watched Cody change.

"Fuck this shii—aaaahhh!"

Another Shock.

"I ain't playing with ya'll any---aaaaahhhhh!!!!"

Another Shock.

"This isn't fair I didn't even---AAAAHHH!!!"

Another Shock.

"Please I don't want…aaaaahhh!"

Another Shock.

The voice repeated the command, "No Talking In The Hallways Please. Please Comply to avoid consequences."

"I Don't under—aaaahhhh!!!!"

Another Shock.

"Dude Just Shut the Fuck Up", yelled another resident from near the front of the line, and he too was administered a shock, briefly. He fell to the ground, and quickly stood back in line, lowering his head to signify that he had understood and is now in compliance, a signal to no one in particular. Cody had understood and stood up silently now, holding in his waning pain and wiping his snot and tears from his face. He looked over at Mack. Mack looked toward the walls, away from everyone, hiding from the situation, and himself. Cody's yellow line began to turn into one straight uninterrupted line again and pulse, while Mack's brown line did the same. The two groups passed each other in silence.

The bright yellow line led Shakeem and the other residents to a large door marked DINING HALL, and the residents waited in silence. Shakeem's stomach growled as he looked at the steel reinforced door. He anticipated a regular regiment of food, nothing out of the ordinary, but his appetite was returning in full force after losing it moments before. Something about his peers being shocked to near paralysis made his hunger diminish. However, now he felt his human urges return. The door slowly began to open as a slightly different voice, a newer recording perhaps, spoke from within the dining hall ceiling.

"Good Morning Residents. Please keep the line orderly and select your breakfast items from the vending machine. Take your seat and enjoy your breakfast. Remember, once you cross the black line into the eating area you may not leave until it is time to do so. To leave the designated area before your time will result in consequences."

This message played three times, with a small ‘ding’ between them. While Shakeem knew exactly where the designations were and had a good idea of where to sit, the new intakes looked cautiously and nervously around the room, straining their necks to see the entire floor without stepping off the line as they shuffled into the room. Immediately to the left of the door was the vending line. They were to step up to the machine, place their fingerprint and select one of the options from the first machine. The small slot below would deliver the item onto a small waiting tray. The next machine would be similar, and administer a different item. Each item was sealed in a plastic-like wrap, even the fruits and vegetables. Immediately in front of the door was the seating area. Each table had four chairs around it, all attached to the floor. The room was only large enough to seat a single pod of residents, so only a few seats were empty by the time every resident shuffled through the line. Once the residents made it through the vending assembly, they followed the pulsing yellow line to the black perpendicular line. With some hesitation, they stepped over the threshold, into free space. They could now walk on their own without any line to follow to find the seat of their choice. The black line surrounded the entire seating area, and only on the other side of the entrance was the familiar line pattern for where they would regroup to leave the hall.

Beyond the seating area was a wall of glass-like material. Beyond this window was the outdoors. Bright sunshine shone through the window mixed with the hues of orange, red, and blue of a morning autumn sky. The grass looked green and inviting, while only small groups of leaves fell around the few trees scattered throughout the landscape. There were a few park benches complete with tables that one could easily sit on and enjoy the morning, midday, or evening meal. The new intakes thought the view to be breathtaking, and as they sat to eat, they stared off into the distance, imagining the day they'll be able to set out there to eat, talk, laugh, and live.

Shakeem looked at his tray. He noticed one of the intakes sitting quietly next to him, looking around in awe and anxiety.

"Hey." Shakeem said, nodding to the new guy. "You can speak in here you know; they don't shock you for talking during meals".

"Oh, yeah… of course," the new intake stammered not sure if he believed it himself, the image of his peers writhing on the floor just moments ago, "I mean, we still can't say *everything* or *anything* we want though, right? We still have to be careful."

Shakeem leaned back in his chair and let out a large belch. The intake's eyes widened, partially impressed by the boldness, partially awaiting some form of immediate punishment.

"I'm going to screw your mother with an axe, the sharp side, and then I'll probably blow up a hospital and stab every one of these fucking kids if I don't get another piece of toast." Shakeem said, in a monotone voice staring directly at the intake.

The new guy, after a moment of silence, waiting, and Shakeem raising his eyebrows to invite a response, said, "Right, in the free movement zones we can say what we want… just not during movement".

Shakeem, satisfied by the answer, nodded and leaned forward again to eat his oatmeal. "What is your name," he said, more as a statement than a question.

"I'm Shawn, uh… resident 6301"

"I don't care about numbers, Shawn."

Shawn was quiet.

Shakeem chewed without speaking for some time, and Shawn's eye started to gaze back toward the window. Shakeem noticed, and smirked, nudging Shawn's tray just a bit with his elbow, "You like that view huh?"

Shawn nodded, "All I've seen so far is concrete, metal doors, and glowing guide lines, it really makes me want to get released as soon as possible."

Shakeem smiled, "Yeah? Getting released to get out there, maybe read a relaxing book, kiss a pretty girl?"

Shawn laughed a little, "Ha, yeah, maybe…"

"It's not real you know," Shakeem dropped his intonation and finished is oatmeal. "It's just a picture they project onto the screen."

Shawn stopped smiling, "W-What do you mean?"

Shakeem laughed sarcastically, "Seriously man, you have to wise up. Why would they put a picture of a meadow outside a dining hall behind a giant glass window?"

"I don't know…" Shawn thought for a moment, "So we have something to hope for? Why would it be fake?"

Shakeem sighed and looked around, and then whispered, more to himself than to Shawn, "Everything about this place is fake. Don't trust anything."

Shawn and Shakeem ate silently for the rest of the period. Shawn looked a little closer at the people eating, laughing, and talking. He stared a bit harder at the tiles on the walls or the floor. He examined the odd glimmer to the packages around his food. He looked harder at the window partitioning him and the outside world. He snuck glances at the speakers on the walls and the vending machines by the entrance, and he stared a bit longer at the array of thousands of tiny cameras or sensors covering the ceiling looking down on him from above.

After thirty minutes of eating, the speakers instructed the residents to line up, and they again followed the guidelines out of the free-roam area. They collected their trash and trays and passed by a slot in the wall marked “waste” where they were to shove their unused food items and containers. Shawn closely followed Shakeem’s lead.

They entered the hallway, following a glowing pink line, this time, to the education pavilion. They walked, in silence, down the hall passing other groups heading into the cafeteria. The line passed the large metal door leading into their cluster and continued past other various rooms. Shawn read them in his head, mouthing the words as he passed, “Treatment… Room”, he said silently. “Commissary…” he said slowly in his head. The large plain, yet bold, letters stood out to him as ominous, although they, on their own, were nothing but labels. To Shawn, they could have been torture chambers, or perhaps just comfortable rooms with cocoa and candy. Shawn didn’t quite know what to make of the place. He just knew he didn’t want to be shocked… again.

Shakeem and the other residents, with Shawn following behind him, reached the end of the hallway passing a door that said, “Recreation”, and stood silently in front of the “Education Pavilion”. Today was Shawn’s first day at school, a day his mother would usually take photos and help him dress. Today, however, he was alone. He dressed under the eyes of cameras, and cameras were taking pictures of him constantly as he prepared for his ‘big day’ as his mother called the other first days of school. But today he knew he was without her, and he knew it was his fault. Shawn felt tears bubble up inside of him and drip out the side of his eyes and down his cheek. He dared not make a sound in the hallway, but in knowing how his mother must be feeling he almost felt like dying right then and there. The doors began to slide open, and the line moved forward.

The education pavilion was split into six different classes along with a central area called the library. The first room on the left was English, where some student's collars changed colors and they followed the guideline into the assigned room. The line continued forward until it reached Mathematics, where again, some collars would change colors to represent the guideline on the ground, and they would scurry to join that class room. The next class was Science, and this time the collars changed, but a resident was not paying attention. He was still looking into the window of the Mathematics room when the shock started. It was a quick shock, nothing terrible. It immediately forced the resident to pay attention, and he did. Without a large show, he straightened himself, noticed he was the last one to enter the science room, and within three steps placed himself onto the correct line. The primary line continued to History, where the pattern repeated. When the guideline reached the Computer Lab, Shakeem and Shawn's collars lit up, and they stepped quickly into the room, where they were pleased to see a black line surrounding the room: a free-roam area. Along with the other residents who stepped into the room, they relaxed their shoulders, thankful that the walk from the cafeteria to education was quick and painless. Everything was better when everyone followed the rules. Shawn and Shakeem found their seats as the speaker on the ceiling, nestled between thousands of tiny cameras looking down at them, started to give out instructions. The room was medium sized, and there were only 16 chairs available. The desks fit two residents each, and upon each desk a designated spot where a computer screen and keyboard were embedded into the surface. The immovable screen and keyboard forced the residents to sit three feet apart, and face the proper direction, toward the front of the classroom, where a large screen was placed. The speakers greeted everyone, in a somewhat friendlier, livelier voice, but with undertones of programming and electrical feedback. As with every morning, the voice explained the class expectations, that expression is a great tool for learning, and that inappropriate talk and behavior would result in consequences. Shakeem knew the speech by heart, and let his gaze wander around the room, while Shawn carefully studied every inch of the class, careful not to touch or say anything until he heard every single instruction. Soon the screen flickered on, and standing in front of them was a woman, with a classroom similar to theirs behind her. Shawn thought it looked like a mirror image, where the screen merely reflected their own classroom, or perhaps a portal to another world, where this woman stood between the two. The virtual classroom had its own residents, unfamiliar faces, but roughly the same age. They were mixed in gender and race, and had one significant difference that Shawn recognized a bit slowly. They had no collars on. He touched his own collar, somewhat from shock of his realization, and then quickly put his hand down. Shakeem looked over at Shawn, and whispered, “Don’t play with that thing, pay attention”.

Shawn nodded, and tried to focus as the simulated teacher began teaching both classes. She explained that a certain combination on the keyboard would allow them to ask questions which would be answered immediately or at a later date depending on the nature of the question. Shawn had so many questions, he wondered if they would be appropriate for a simulated computer science teacher. He decided to do nothing, nothing but stare… for now.

The judge looked down at Shawn that afternoon and gave a wiry smile. He said in a deep, kind, deceptively kind, now that Shawn thought about it, voice, “I’ll give you a choice young man. Clearly you lack your own proper decision-making skills, or you would not be in this court room. Clearly your parents have not been able to teach you right from wrong, and clearly you haven’t been able to learn how to control your own body. But you’re still fairly young, and I believe there can be something in you to salvage, something for you to offer society. So, I give you the choice. The Paris School of Rehabilitation, or Prison?”

Shawn looked around the court room. He was standing next to his public defender, a pretty young woman who was also new to this situation. She gently put her hand on his shoulder as if to say, ‘it’s up to you’. And Shawn felt as if this choice wouldn’t change much. He leaned into the small microphone on the desk in front of him and said,

“Um, your honor, I would rather go to the School than to Prison”. The public defender gently patted him on the back, as if to say, ‘good choice’, but when Shawn looked over with a grin, all he saw in return was an avoidant gaze. She quickly looked away from him. His countenance fell as he turned back to the judge wondering what the consequence was for his last, perhaps terrible, decision. The judge smiled differently now. He was eager.

“Very well. For the crimes committed by you, armed robbery with an unauthorized firearm as well as 12 counts of burglary and assault with a class G weapon outside of the district, in addition to 73 counts of truancy, and 21 counts of illegal drug possession with the intent to distribute, I sentence you to 18 months mandatory to the Paris School of Rehabilitation. The exact date of your release will be determinant on your behavior at the facility and by their internal system after 18 months." He pounded his gavel twice, "Good luck."

Shawn's heart sank. He knew, still, it would be better than prison. He knew the stories his father had told him before he was shot. He heard how the men there would do horrible things to each other, and the guards would join in or gamble on which prisoner would win or lose. He knew he wouldn't be safe in prison, but the smile on the judge's face made his stomach queasy.

Once the court room cleared, two uniformed police officers led Shawn down a hallway in handcuffs and shackles and out two steel doors that led directly to the back of the courthouse. There was a chanting going on that Shawn could hear from the side of the street. Protesters were there to complain about the new cloning facility that opened up recently. Before Shawn could hear exactly what they were saying he was pushed through another set of doors. There was the truck; an old-fashioned armored vehicle that had a cab attached to the back. As one officer took off the shackles, the other opened the doors to reveal other teenagers waiting in the truck. They looked angry, and mostly sad. One even seemed to have been crying. Shawn climbed in as the officers confirmed he was the last case. The door slammed closed, and Shawn was alone with his peers. Obviously, they looked at each other, but only in secret. The other boys saw Shawn as a lanky kid, a mix of black and white with brown hair and glasses. He wasn't particularly tall, perhaps just under average for his age.

He gave an aura of passive denial, the type of person who could abstain any information until you believed he might be telling the truth. Shawn had gotten by on his con-artist abilities, the ability to trick the system, to trick the faulty human mind into believing they knew less than he did. That's how he moved the drugs from under one supplier's nose to the buyer without the cops thinking twice. That's how he could slip past the suspicions of the guards at the mall or any restaurant. He could always fool a person if they were half human. It was so instinctual to him that he began playing the 'comforter' as soon as he felt eyes glare at him in the truck. Once the doors closed and the loud locking sounds stopped from just outside the door, he started the 'it'll be alright if we stick together' speech. Shawn knew how these situations worked. Everyone needed to be the toughest, so everyone was waiting to trump the other. If Shawn were to say he was the 'baddest mother fucker' in the truck, surely another kid would challenge, and he'd have to prove it. If he were to pretend he didn't exist, eventually the other kids would assume he was an easy target. If he acted like he could offer them something, a way out, or some sort of supplies, he would be seen as a supplier, but eventually he would be manipulated into being used. He thought this out and came to the conclusion, he had to get everyone on the same team.

"Hey… hey." He whispered in a cool, but commanding voice.

"Shut up man, we don't want to hear it", another kid said in the corner.

"Look, we all know where we're going. We all know we did bad shit, it's whatever. We have to keep ourselves together okay?" Shawn said, making it seem that he was mostly talking to himself. This gave those who truly didn't care permission to ignore him, and those who pretended not to care permission to pretend to ignore him. He continued after some silence, meaning everyone was listening now.

"If we let them see us cry, or let them see us fall apart, then they win. They can try to change us, to *rehabilitate* us all they want, but **we** know who we are. **WE** know what we stand for, and we're not going to let them take what's inside of us, not who we are inside. Right?" He looked around the room, with a soft but determined face. He crafted this look the first time his father caught him with stolen merchandise. After his initial lies failed, and his father was about to beat him as usual, he looked at his dad with this soft, yet determined face, as if to say to him, "Do what you want to me, but these are my decisions. I am a man and this is my life!". This humble assertiveness generally allowed him out of harsh punishments. There were no beatings that day, but after a long, long talk, they even shook hands: the diploma of a senior manipulator.

The teenagers in the truck looked at Shawn now, with the same softness. While each of them wondered how they were going to play the toughest guy in school, Shawn gave them an out. They could work together, rely on each other, rather than resist. Shawn gave them an enemy, the guards, and the teachers. 'They couldn't change us if they wanted to.' 'We're too strong and awesome.' 'We're fine as we are. 'We just have to stay who we are and not get distracted,' the kids thought as the truck began to rumble and roll onward.

"Right." The kids said.

Shawn shifted his weight in his seat on the truck and dared not smile, although he was elated that his plan was working. All he had to do next was get into the good graces of the guards at the facility, his mandatory 18 months would become 12 soon. He spent the rest of the ride learning particulars about the new intakes, and just what was useful or detrimental about each one.

Shawn was confident when he stepped off the truck with his fellow allies and was greeted by a liaison inside of the building. He was not able to get a glimpse of the outside of the facility because the truck backed into the loading area labeled 'Intake'. All he could see was the desk in front of him and the kindly older woman sitting behind it. His allies behind him in line, and two security guards with rifles standing passively by. The lady welcomed the group and mentioned that they would have to do some screening.

"The screening will be done quickly; in fact, you won't be aware of most of it. Part of the process is a small semi-invasive procedure which is standard policy here at the Paris School. Please follow me!" She seemed overly cheery for someone her age, thought Shawn. They followed her, still in handcuffs to another room where separate attendants took the individuals to separate beds. It reminded them of a hospital operating room. Each attendant held a small vial of blue thick liquid and the residents were to drink the entire vial as quickly as they could. Shawn noted that the attendants said very little, and it was very difficult to find an opening in which to make a quip or show his charm. Shawn felt a twinge of anxiety.

He drank his liquid, and it tasted metallic and sweet, like overly sweetened medicine. One of the other inmates exclaimed "Yuck, what is this shit?". The attendant made no attempts to console him, but instead insisted that he finish the entire vial. The specific instructions were direct.

“Finish the vial.” One of the armed guards escorting the group looked over at the resident curiously. The inmate winced, but complied. They were all told to lay on the operation tables, and they did. They were comfortable, and for the first time Shawn noted how tired he was from the day’s excitement. He stayed still as the attendants and guards left the room. Shawn, in his comfort, barely recognized that he was in fact alone with the other residents for the first time. His last thought, as he drifted to sleep was, “not a smart facility at all…”. Darkness swallowed him.

Shawn, along with the new intakes awoke in chairs. They were in a small living space with a large visible speaker and a large security camera behind scratched glass, or some sort of hard plastic. Shawn quickly looked around, attempting to recall what had happened since he was last awake. He twisted his head back and forth just to note that there was something interrupting his normal movement. He had a collar on. They all had collars on. While thin enough he could move his neck in all directions, they were tight enough that one could not forget they were there. They were wearing new clothes, and everything that was on them at the time was missing. He immediately began trying to loosen the collar and speak, “Hey, what happened to us?” said another inmate, just before Shawn could ask a similar question.

“I have no idea,” murmured another inmate, “I just woke up”.

“What the fuck man—" another resident was in the middle of exclaiming when he suddenly stopped speaking. He clutched his throat and held his chest as he writhed and fell to the floor, gasping for breath. The speaker in front of them on the wall stated in a pleasant female voice, “Please, no cursing is allowed at Paris”.

The resident nodded and his pain seemed to subside as he slowly stopped clutching his body.
“Wait, Wait, What the fuck is—" another resident fell to the same mistake, and similarly his body began to convulse.
“Please, no cursing is allowed at Paris”
“Cut this Shit ou—" another resident.
“Please, no cursing is allowed at Paris”
“What the fu—"
“Please, no cursing is allowed at Paris”
“Guys…” Shawn said at last, after watching the painful pattern, “Just shut up for a minute”.
Shawn had to think, and seeing his peers groan, gasp, and clutch for their lives was distracting him. The collars, the blue liquid, the feeling of being well rested, but groggy; they must have been knocked out and had something done to them. He didn’t understand exactly what happened.
“If we curse, we get shocked or something?” Shawn said this to the camera watching the room, he thought of old shock collars they used for training animals. The speaker replied, “If a rule is broken, there will be consequences. Are there any other questions?”
The new intakes started to talk at once, “What rules?” “Where are we?” “Where the Fuc—ahhhhh” “This can’t be legal” “I want my Fuc—aahhh” “Where is the warden?”
Consequences were administered accordingly, and then the voice continued. “The rules you will find out as you continue through the program. The consequences will be your guide. You are at the Paris School Rehabilitation Program within the intake pavilion. This is an area

where you can test out our protocols and ask your questions. To begin, there is a limited number of staff employed at the program facility. To reduce inefficiency in our cognitive behavioral model we have eliminated human error. There will always be a camera and sensors in your vicinity to monitor all resident behavior and speech as well as make judgements about thought patterns and other mental or psychological issues. Based on your behavior there may be different severities of consequences which are regulated through your collars. Please do not attempt to remove your collars for that will surely result in more dire consequences. Are there any questions so far?"

After this speech, the residents were all quiet. They looked at Shawn, the only one who had not been given a consequence yet. Shawn looked around and quietly asked, "How will we know where to go… or what to do without any human direction?" Shawn did not want the answer to this question.

The camera seemed to flicker and the speaker seemed to give feedback of some sort as a bright purple line on the ground lit up. Small lights on each of the new intake's collars lit up as their shirts reflected the purple color. "Please follow all directives, and proceed where directed in a timely manner. You will follow the guidelines that are lit up and correspond to your collar's color." As if by precognition the speaker stopped speaking and with another instance of electrical feedback interjected immediately after the statement, "We have tested you all for color blindness and your eyes are fully capable of telling the colors apart from each other", a sentiment that Shawn had only recently begun to think of.

Shawn began to sweat. He was being analyzed by a mechanism that knew him before he had a chance to think himself: he was trying to find a way to delegitimize following a meaningless arbitrary rule, something disqualifying such as a disability. What would qualify him to be different from the others, maybe some defect; he would have eventually considered color blindness as an easy condition to fake, and once he was tested, he would be able to have special circumstances, and maybe even form an escape plan. All of this was dismissed before he had a chance to even think of it himself. Shawn began to recognize his own fear. He was going to be locked up. This was real. His fear became a panic.

"Please step on the purple line, left foot securely on the line with your right foot within shoulder's length." The speaker stated calmly.

Still indignant, two residents refused, stating they would not be bossed around by a voice in a box. The others, learning their lesson stood on the guideline that was lit up. Within a few seconds the two residents who failed to comply changed their minds, after a period of screaming and writhing on the ground by the lines.

Shawn found himself marching along in a small trail with his intake peers. He stopped when the speaker told him to. He learned to stop if the guidelines were fragmented rather than solid. He understood what the speaker meant by free-roaming within a black square, which existed in the corner of this intake processing room. He decided, after marching around like a trained pet, at last to show one last sign of rebellion at the fingerprint scanner.

"Please place your finger on the fingerprint scanner to exit the intake room as your orientation to the security and order portion of the

Paris facility is complete." The purple line lit up and led the intakes to the door where there was a small console. A single finger could be placed on the lit-up box that showed a small image of which finger to place. Shawn had to resist. He felt that with this one act he would be, if he hadn't already, be signing his life away to a robot. He took one last look at the small image of himself, his name and in bold the numbers 6301. He couldn't help but smirk as he stepped off the line.

"Please stay on the line to process your finger print". The speaker immediately stated the directive. Shawn said nothing. His peers began to murmur, "Please dude, common".

Before Shawn could say anything, it started. The pain started in his legs, they tightened immediately knocking him to the floor. The heat radiated upward and into his genitals, making his breathing tight and hollow. He found himself gasping for breath as he reached out to nothing in particular. His chest tightened as his heart seemed to beat out of his chest while the shocks continued to pierce his skin from all sides. His blood felt as if it was made of spikes that pierced every nerve in his body. He wanted to rip apart his own body from the inside out but suddenly it stopped. No pain whatsoever. His collar pulsed the color and the purple line was within his grasp, and he quickly crawled over to it, and stood up, cautious for any lingering effects of the consequence. There was none.

"Please place your finger on the console to process your fingerprint." The voice stated as calmly as before, as if nothing had happened.

"Torture", Shawn thought. "This is torture." He put his finger on the scanner, his name slowly disappeared as the numbers remained, and the line pulsed once more. The door opened to the main hallway. The intakes stepped out onto the hallway, careful to follow the purple line as indicated by their collar's color and the glow of the guideline. The hallway was empty, but soon they were led to a large metal door labeled, "Living Cluster". He waited for the door to open in silence, as instructed by the new speaker on the ceiling and walls. He casually peered around himself from time to time, still not sure what was allowed and what wasn't. He noticed the thousands of little dark spots all along the ceiling and upper part of the hallway walls, out of reach. He knew they were cameras, watching, judging, analyzing, and concluding on what he was about to do, what he was thinking, and what consequence could be given out next. Shawn thought of the feeling of his blood stabbing him from within again and stopped looking around. He only looked down.

The Living Cluster doors opened and the purple line led him toward the center of the cluster. His collar lit up and was now green. He noted that the person in front of him and behind him were given other colors as well while corresponding guidelines lit up around them. There was no time for good bye, or a rousing speech about sticking together. There was no charismatic charm from Shawn to keep up the good graces of the furious bunch who would never let anyone take what they had. There was no cohort, no army, and no allies. For now, they didn't have even the luxury to cry as they parted ways and followed their lines meticulously to their assigned pods scattered across the cluster. They had their collars, their colors, their lines, and their instructions.

Shawn's line led him to a room with a barcode over where a number might have been a long time ago. He placed his finger on the small console outside the room where his number 6301 glowed as the door opened and the green line behind him faded. He was relieved to see the black line surround the outside perimeter of his room, a free-roam space. He, while cautious, took a wide step into the area and inspected his lodging. He wanted to feel alone, he needed to think. He needed to process all of this. He was drugged, probably operated on, maybe even violated in some way. He had to contact someone or escape somehow. He had a long list of elements to consider and he might have done so if he did not notice the large speaker and camera staring at him, mounted on the wall by the door.

"Welcome, Shawn, resident 6301", the voice from the localized speaker said. "You seem to have a lot on your mind. Your profile matches that of a thinker. If you require any more information, press the button under the speaker that will activate the microphone, and this will add your query to the main index where your question will be answered at the earliest convenience. Welcome to Paris, 6301." *Shawn* was always stated oddly, as if that portion of the recording was added recently by a slightly different recorded voice. Shawn went to the bed and sat on it. He looked toward the window, showing a generic field, nothing for miles. He looked at this desk, attached to the wall with a stool that seemed to be attached to the desk. He looked at the door that had since his entrance closed behind him. He then looked back to the glaring camera.

"We will be enemies, you and I. I will study and consider everything I have the power to study, and I will beat you. You think you have control of me, but I will break out of this place and I will murder you for what you've done to me. I do not care if it kills me, I will break every fucking bone in my body if I have to. But I will leave here." Shawn thought.

"Please rest now, Shawn, 6301. It has been a long day." said the speaker, and the lights dimmed in the room. Shawn was not amused.

Rehabilitation

Larry followed the bright pink line down the hallway and stopped at the door labeled Treatment Room. When everyone stopped behind him the door opened and they followed that main line into the expected waiting area. They stood on the pink line now in profile, all facing doors that lead to their individual treatment rooms for counseling. This was the only time during the week where outside human contact was permitted, and this was always every resident's favorite portion of the day. After treatment was complete for the day, however, the residents were often the most depressed. As they stood, one by one their colors would change, a new guide line to a specific door would appear, and the resident would quickly shuffle to the door. The door would open and the resident would eagerly rush inside. The speaker would explain this process intermittently until each resident was behind their assigned doors. The atmosphere in the waiting room was unnerving in a way. Each resident was eager to get into their rooms, each resident waiting quietly, not wishing to waste their breath on mindless conversation with a peer even if they were allowed to. However, the most nerve-wracking possibility was if treatment time was cancelled. The resident would be the last one waiting for their line to brighten up with color, but instead there would be nothing. The main treatment room door would reopen and another line would lead the resident back to the cluster or some other activity area. The resident could choose to throw a tantrum, which could result in a severe consequence, or the resident would slowly, quietly, shuffle back out the room, into the hallway, and onto an alternative activity.

Larry was not nervous, however. He was excited. His release date was next week and he was finally going to rejoin society. As his green line lit up and led him to one of the middle doors within the treatment room, he stepped confidently with his head held high. He stepped to the door as it opened and continued to follow the green line into the counseling room. The counseling rooms were mysterious and quite interesting to residents. Directly across from the door Larry entered through there was another door, but this one with a handle. Between the two doors there was a desk and two chairs, one on each side of the desk, but none connected to the floor. The wall to one side contained a couch, and the other side held panels, some able to be activated by the treatment specialist, and some merely part of the wall. The resident could not tell which panel held an item, and which panel was decorative. In addition to all of this, there was, of course, not a sea of cameras on the ceiling, as in every other portion of the building, but only one, along with a speaker. Larry smiled as he stepped in, recognizing the room from his months of incarceration. He had used each counseling room, almost never using the same one twice in a row, but he did prefer this particular one. The chairs seemed softer, and the space was a tad bit bigger. He liked the smell, although he may have imagined all these things, he enjoyed his own bias, rather than hiding from it. He stepped over the black line that did not go around to each corner of the room, but instead a large circle around the desk and the chair in the center of the room. Outside of this circle there were yellow diagonal lines stretching from the black circle to the corners of the room. These areas, Larry knew, a resident should never step in. As he walked to the chair and sat down, settling himself and playfully tapping on the desk in front of him, he started to laugh to himself. When he first arrived, he was a much different person. Almost 24 months had passed since he was sentenced to the Paris School, and for most of those months he refused to do any work on himself whatsoever. He refused to eat any more than what yielded a consequence, refused to participate in recreation, and refused treatment. Whenever he could show defiance he chose to, and whenever he could deny the 'system' information he would do so. Something changed, however, for Larry, and Larry finally started to work harder.

The secondary door opened suddenly and a man stepped out of the darkened door. "Hey Larry, how are you doing?" The man was short, much shorter than Larry who stood at 6' 1", and much stockier and out of shape. He took a few steps to the chair opposite to Larry at the desk and sat down in a huff. Larry replied eagerly, and with a smile, "Hey Mr. Jones! I'm doing well! One more week, right?"

"One more week." Mr. Jones repeated, his tone changing from social to practical, "Any consequences this week?" Mr. Jones began writing on a few of the papers within a folder he had brought with him.

"Haha," Larry chuckled, "I haven't had a consequence in months. No problem!"

"Any violent thoughts?"

"Not really, I had a bad dream about a building on fire," Larry said, and then added, "But I didn't set the building on fire."

"Any other dreams, Larry?"

"Nothing interesting, just the usual…" Larry trailed off and began listing some elements, "… family, girls, a job…"

“What are your plans when you get released, Larry.” Mr. Jones seemed to say this as a statement, not a question.

“I plan on earning my education, staying focused in my work, and help contribute to society in any way I know how, Sir.” Larry smiled as he repeated the words from memory.

Mr. Jones looked up from his papers just as he finished signing his name on the summary form and scratched a little at his wrist. He was wearing a bracelet that matched the style of the resident’s collar. The bracelet was tight, but looser than the resident’s, so it moved slightly around his wrist and caused some discomfort. Mr. Jones smiled at Larry, “Good enough.” He turned his wrist and pressed a few buttons on his bracelet. There was a whirr in the room, and the speaker in the ceiling chimed, “Camera Deactivated”.

Larry slammed his hands down on the table in excitement and stood up. He stretched, and let out a loud groan as if waking up from a comfortable nap. Mr. Jones stood up as well, watching Larry exaggerate. They both laughed and walked to the couch to relax. Larry immediately began asking questions,

“So, dude, how is my mom doing? And my sister? Did she get those new shoes like she’s been wanting?”

Mr. Jones replied with an update on the family and his life as Larry existed absent from it. Larry would ask about the celebrity gossip, how his favorite basketball team was doing, if his court documents were in order, or if his girlfriend was still around. He would ask age-appropriate questions, such as how sexy one actress or new pop-star was, and even make a request for Mr. Jones to describe his last meal. In addition to regular treatment, as the treatment specialist saw fit, the resident was allowed to vent about anything, learn about the world, get the updates on politics, hear about what has happened on the outside of the facility, and for a brief moment believe they are part of a civilization again.

Mr. Jones stood up and walked to the other side of the room after Larry began laughing at one of his own stories. Jones walked to the array of small panels on the wall and pressed another button on his bracelet. One panel made a 'hiss' as the hydraulic system activated and the panel was ejected outward, slowly, revealing a small drawer. Jones reached inside and pulled out a photograph. The panel automatically closed once Jones' fingers were out of the way. Larry sat upright, watching all of this extremely eager to see what the item was.

"Larry, I know these last two years were difficult for you. I know they were especially difficult after you received the extension."

"Never try to kill yourself, it only makes life worse," Larry chimed in.

"Right. But I think in a few ways the extension was good for you. It gave us a bit more time to work on some of these issues and I believe you're in a good place."

Larry nodded, still trying to see what was in Mr. Jones' hand.

"So, I'm going to apologize for not telling you this earlier, but I thought it was better to tell you now, rather than earlier. Forgive me."

Larry swallowed the lump in his throat, and looked eagerly at the picture Jones held out in front of him. Larry took the photo and leaned back in the couch, and began to weep, tears streaming down his cheeks to his neck, and around his collar onto his shirt, never taking his eyes off the photo. His girlfriend, mother, sister, and a little girl, about 1years old holding his girlfriend's hand, waving at the camera. Larry placed a hand over his mouth and asked the question, "Who is the little girl?"

"Your girlfriend named her Monica. She's your daughter."

Mr. Jones let Larry weep, in sadness and in joy until the time was up. The small speaker in Mr. Jones' bracelet rang twice indicating the time was nearly complete. Larry composed himself and sat back at the table. Still wiping away tears, Jones reactivated the cameras with confirmation of the speakers, and they concluded their session.

"Resident has shown progress with his treatment and has reduction of the prevailing ailments of anger and aggression, tendency to harm others, tendency to commit violent crimes, and lack of empathy. Client shows progress and I formally request termination upon completion of the Paris program in accordance with legislation and judicial oversight. End of treatment session. Jones." Mr. Jones read the paper out loud for Larry to hear, and placed the paper back into his folder. Larry nodded along, but stared at the picture in his hand. Mr. Jones smiled at Larry, "It's yours, and I'll bring in a few more the next time I visit, probably in a few days before you are formally discharged. That meeting will be even less formal, and I plan to have the paper work all complete before then. After that you'll be out of here. Good work Mr. Larry."

Larry nodded, "Thank you for everything Mr. Jones".

The light on the guideline lit up again, the same green line from before. Larry automatically stood up, and followed the line, looking back once more at Mr. Jones smiling as he waited by his secondary door entrance. Larry took a few steps to the door, it opened, and Larry found himself in the waiting room again, just as the other residents were lining up once more on their pink waiting line. They all shuffled slowly back to the line, much more sluggish than they arrived. Some had items in their hands such as a small trinket from a family member, or a photograph to keep in their rooms. Some just smiled to themselves, and others had a look of determination or pure focus on their faces. Their treatment was complete for the day and it was time to return to the facility for now.

The Sad Case of Sam

Sam wasn't a bad kid; he was just forgetful. He would run around and play with his friends and just forget that his mom told him to be in before nine o'clock. He would be reminded at some point, and rush home in a hurry, always too late, and always receive a punishment, some harsher than others. After a day of forgetting, however, the story would start over again. In school it was the same. "Be sure to do chapters 3 and 4 for homework tonight," the teacher would write down on the board as she read her instructions out loud. Sam would write the instructions down in his notebook. While the class was shuffling out of the room the teacher would also verbally remind everyone to do the short answer questions at the end of each chapter; an assumed end to a reading assignment. They all groaned, including Sam. After hours of video games, playing football with his friends in the park, and finally noticing the time, Sam would rush home to do his homework. He would read the words on his to do list, read the chapters as he was instructed to do, and forget everything else. In class everyone would be handing in papers and then Sam would remember. Unfortunately. Sam wasn't just forgetful, he remembered at the wrong time. Sam remembered after it was too late, and being an honest person, he could no longer use the excuse, "I don't remember". He could attempt to explain his situation and express exactly when he forgot and when he regained his recollection, however this always sounded more like an excuse than reality, and results were never any good.

"Where is your homework Sam." The teacher would ask without a question mark.

"Well, I read the chapters…"

"Don't you remember what I said just before class was let out yesterday?" This was the earnest question.

"Yes… I do now… but when I got home yesterday, I forgot" Sam tried to explain.

"So, you didn't remember when you were playing, but now, suddenly, you remember. Do we need to have another talk with your mother?" This wasn't a real question either, the teacher had already made plans to call after the last test was marked a 'D-'. This was merely a way to make Sam feel uncomfortable, to make the other students recognize what a failure looked like, at least this is what Sam thought.

"I didn't mean to forget! Why do you have to call my mom!?" Sam responded

"I'm not sure if you're going to make it to the next grade with this attitude, Sam" the teacher said quietly, looking over the classroom of students. Some children started to snicker and giggle as Sam began to get more and more embarrassed and upset.

This is where Sam made his mistake. He felt like running out of the room's door, or sitting down and crying, or even throwing a pencil at the teacher. He instead turned to the window and opened it. Sam was going to jump out. Within an instant, and with some gasps from the students around him, the teacher yelled, "Close that window! Sam! You're going to get hurt!". The teacher ran to the window just as Sam was about to step out onto the ledge. Sam was too angry to listen, and too embarrassed to step back into the classroom. Why should he sit there to be ridiculed? He needed to leave, so he was leaving the easiest way possible.

The teacher grabbed onto his pant leg just as he was about to jump out. Sam's leg along with the upper half of the teacher's torso exited the window. As the teacher's neck strained to hold on, Sam kicked with his other foot screaming, "LET ME GO", his shoe smashed the teacher's nose inward, and the back of her head hit the window pane just as she let go of Sam. The rumble of contact made the locking mechanism of the window become undone, and the window fell onto the teacher's neck, trapping her as well as severing her spinal cord. Sam landed with both hands and feet onto the ground and turned to look back at the second-floor window of his small high school, and saw the blood of his teacher fall after him. Sam would be charged with battery, along with acts of disturbing the peace, destroying school property, truancy, and failing to answer the short answer questions after reading chapters 3 and 4.

In court the judge seemed to understand that it was all an accident, all a matter of circumstance. There was no previous record of violence or deviations from the social contract in Sam's past. He was terrible at school, but as Sam attempted to explain to the judge, with the help of his mother, Sam was merely forgetful, and this caused many, many issues for him. Counseling wasn't helpful, the mother stated in court, because Sam would often forget what the counselors said anyway, and medications were not developed enough to help Sam with his issues. The judge sentenced Sam to the Paris School for Boys to serve his sentence and to also gain some behavioral modification to help him remember better. The judge kindly took the time to explain that there he would be monitored and his memory problems would be easily corrected by the use of a behaviorism model. Sam's mother did not understand, but liked the idea of Sam learning how to modify his memory issues for the better. While she had no say in the matter, she still made a point to agree with the judge and willingly send her son to Paris. Sam just thought he needed a pad and paper to write more notes in from time to time, but no one asked Sam.

Sam stumbled. Sam fell. Sam's consequences were Hell. After a short time, Sam wanted to die. He didn't remember to look at the changing colors, or sometimes which direction he was going. He would hear the speakers say one thing, but would forget just as quickly and do something else. Consequence. Sam would see someone he knew or wanted to ask a question, and would blurt it out in the hallway. Consequence. Sam would step off his line before the guideline would light up. Consequence. Sam would walk over to the vending machine to get another apple 'real quick'. Consequence. Sam would laugh at a joke in class and playfully nudge another resident. Consequence. Sam would lay in bed for much too long. Consequence. Consequence. Consequence.

Sam finally began to learn, though. Sam would see the line change, and control his impulse. He would wait, and move with everyone else. Sam would see someone in the hall, and just before blurting out their name he would cover his mouth. At first Sam would raise his hand as if in school, to ask a question in the hallway. This would slow the line and result in consequence. He then would raise his hand, to whom, he didn't know, but he would raise it while walking. This would not result in consequence; it showed improvement. Soon the consequences would diminish, as he chuckled to himself in classes, and remembered to order his fruit while he was in the line, not afterward. He would recall the place he was going and stay on the right track. When a random event would occur, or when the schedule would change, he was eager to listen, and repeat the overhead message to himself in his own words so he could remember it, rather than ignoring it or forgetting it later. Paired with the strict consequences and the constant redirection, Sam started to see changes in his own behavior; He was earning less consequences, and remembering more fluidly. He could substitute old information for newer information, and rather than cling to his long-term memory, he could better use his short-term and working memory to be more flexible. Sam didn't know it, but Sam was also growing up. Six months would go by quickly, and Sam would already be receiving less consequences. His grades were improving, and his overall enjoyability of life would increase from there. He could clearly think about the future and integrate information from multiple sources at once to create a coherent thought. Sam was progressing well through the program.

Under the watchful eye of the monitors, Sam, along with the other residents, were finally able to focus entirely on their studies and their day-to-day tasks. Sam soon found it was time to be released from Paris, and his skills that were extremely necessary and important within the facility were different from that on the outside. Sam would remain quiet in classrooms, until designated question times, not recognizing that he could ask a question at any time in a college preparatory course. He would try to follow an imaginary line as he walked through the hallways of buildings, growing anxious when the bizarre complex floor patterns of a bank or a mall changed erratically, causing him to briefly expect a moment of intense pain. The anxiety, where for a brief moment his stomach would curl and his feelings would flatten while he attempted to brace himself mentally and emotionally for the coming surge of pain, would only increase over time, rather than dissipate. Soon Sam became paranoid in believing he would get shocked for not waking up at the right time, or going to sleep too late. Being disciplined for behaviors that were not registered in the Paris behavioral archive, such as picking his nose, or coughing too loudly, Sam began to fear as well. While Sam seemed to remember how to remember, he forgot how to forget.

It is rarely reported that a resident leaving the facility has such an adverse reaction. Typically, the central computer has a projection pattern of reducing stimuli and slowly changing the algorithm for consequences in relation to a resident's psychological profile. For some cases, however, there are variables that lead to fatalities. It was about a year later when Sam killed himself. A couple out jogging found him walking down a highway in the early morning, following the yellow line demarcating the breakdown lane. When they tried to ask him if he was okay, or if he needed help, he was startled, stepped off the line, and started screaming at the couple. He shouted something to the effect of, "there are always consequences!", and jumped into traffic, thrusting himself into an oncoming vehicle. Only later was it revealed that Sam was a resident at Paris, and suddenly his statements began to make sense. If only he had answered the short answer questions following chapter 3 and 4.

Investigations into the program began, and it wasn't long before the Paris program was in the papers and on the news. Few changes were made, and since the success rate to fatality rate was so significantly distinct, most aspects were left as they were. Minor warnings were expressed to judges and to the public, and some fine print was changed on a few forms.

Paris, however, stayed exactly the same.

“Things are always the same”, Shakeem stated to no one in particular as he lay in bed, waiting for the automatic lights to turn on in his room. He looked at the fake window, out into the fake scenery outside. He didn’t care enough to get up, but he did enjoy playing a game with himself. He wanted to see how long he could go without a consequence, and he didn’t feel like losing that game either. He toyed with the thought of just lying-in bed, and getting consequence after consequence, just to see how much he could take. As the bell rang, and as the lights turned on, he quickly sobered up from his fantasies, and decided in the end it wasn’t worth it. He decided to continue to be like Larry, while discharged, still a good role model.

Shakeem shuffled in line for some time through the day feeling that there was hardly a point to anything. He used the bathroom at the designated times, and raised his hand at the designated time. He even helped out another resident calm down in the cafeteria when necessary. Shakeem did all this with an unphased attitude. He was becoming numb. When it was time for his weekly treatment, he waited for his treatment counselor to arrive. The appropriate lights changed and he stood in the designated room when his counselor finally arrived. Her name was Karah.

“Hi there Shakeem! It’s good to see you again!” Karah was a young eager fresh-from-college type as Shakeem would put it. She went out of her way to give reasons for things and try to make everything and everyone ‘feel’ better. She listened, in a robotic way, and responded in a scripted way, and bored Shakeem overall.

“Hello.” Shakeem said, taking his seat by the empty desk. Karah had a few papers and files with her, and placed them on the desk. She touched a few buttons on her bracelet and the colors changed slightly. She eventually gave a big exaggerated 'sigh', and smiled at Shakeem as if she accomplished something significant.

"Wow! Okay! Let's get started, shall we? I remember what we talked about last time, and since you're an indefinite commitment your stay will be determined solely by the discretion of the facility central monitoring system!"

Shakeem already knew this, they had talked about this when he was first sentenced, as well as every other week for the past fourteen months. Shakeem raised his eyebrows as if to say, "So?".

"Well, this is exciting! The Central computer is saying that you're just about ready to leave! Maybe this month! Isn't that amazing?" Karah smiled deeply. Shakeem did not.

"Am I leaving this month or not?" Shakeem stated, with flat affect.

"Well, you know that's up to you!", she smiled as if making an inside joke, "As long as you behave well, you should be discharged back to the community in two weeks. Isn't that good news?"

"I've been extended before, for '*unknown variables*. How do I know that won't happen again?" Shakeem didn't change his expression. While he fought the urge to think about finally getting out, the reality of being trapped for yet another month or two, or six, still echoed in his mind. His initial sentence was nine months. He was not going to be easily moved by empty 'good news'.

"Well, this time the information is from the behavioral processing computer, the other times it was from my recommendations corroborated with the court and the psychiatrists I report to. They thought you were ready a while ago, but apparently, we were wrong. When was your last consequence?" Karah melded the two sentences together, as if she didn't want to explain what she meant.

"Two months. What do you mean the processing computer?" Shakeem was curious about what exactly she meant.

"Great, any violent thoughts?" Karah continued.

"No, nothing violent. Which computer is deciding to keep me here?" Shakeem sat up and leaned forward.

"Wonderful, and how are your studies going?" Karah continued.

"They're fine. But, wait a second, how do you know…."

"And you're getting along with the other residents?"

Silence.

Karah waited patiently, still looking at her paper, jotting down notes. Shakeem just waited. He guessed at the game. Was she provoking him? Was she just trying to get through the standardized questions? Did she just not care, or does she just want to leave? Shakeem decided to say nothing. After some time Karah looked up at him and smiled, "I think this was a productive session Shakeem. I look forward to meeting with you again."

Karah stood up, and so did Shakeem. She collected her papers and returned to the door, fidgeting with the buttons on her wrist. Her door opened, and she shuffled out quickly.

Shakeem stood there alone for a moment after her door closed. The black line around his area was still active, so he sat back down. This was the first time, in some time, that there was finally more information. The behavior processing computer said he had to stay, but everyone else thought he should leave. Maybe she wasn't supposed to mention that at all. Maybe she wasn't allowed to tell him this. Shakeem didn't know what to make of it. But like always, Shakeem stayed quiet. Soon his green line lit up, as well as his collar, and he joined the others in the hallway outside the individual treatment rooms. He followed the green line back to the living cluster for free time, but this time, something was different.

Shawn stood in the free time area on the living cluster. The marked area was surrounded by a black line that seemed to be painted on the ground, rather than within the floor as the other lights are. Clearly the lines weren't weighted or tracking anything, just there for the cameras to better track movement, Shawn thought when he first saw them. Shawn's amazement of the building didn't stop despite being within the system's walls for a week now. He took his time studying each order, looking for any gaps of cameras, or any other detail that could be of use. Shawn took his time, and didn't forget his vow from his first night in his room. He will find a way out of this place, he swore it.

Eventually, other residents, following their lines, stepped into the black free time square. Shawn noted a distinct difference between the almost robotic zombie-like way the residents stepped into the square, and then the calm relaxed, human way they sprung to life. Many of the residents slouched a bit more, and made their steps a bit slower. They slid their hands down the front or sides of the pants, due to the lack of pockets, just to rest their arms. They spoke to each other in low tones, sizing each other up, venting a bit, talking about how they couldn't wait to get out of the place. Some, however, stayed as they were before. Perhaps less zombiesque, but still standing straight, refraining from curse words, and generally talking about their education classes and potential works. Shawn quickly noted that the intakes seemed to be the ones more cautious to say anything or loosen up. Some of the intermediate stays, a month or so under their belt, seemed to resist the function of their facility decorum, and regress as soon as they were able to do so. Some of the veterans, however, remained as they were at all times, perhaps considering the extreme amount of effort it would require to both fake a dynamic change from following a line and wandering around the free space, and to pretend to not be used to the basic and simple rules of the facility. Even to Shawn it didn't seem like the program was asking much. Being quiet in the hallways, choosing one's words carefully, and being prompt and on time to appointments and movement wasn't difficult. What exactly was the program going to teach anyone? What was it trying to teach him?

Shawn felt a presence behind him as he watched one of the pink lines fade out as the last resident stepped over the black line and into the square. He turned to see Shakeem who had just stepped off his green line.

"Oh, Hey." Shawn said,

"When are you getting out of here?" Shakeem stated more than asked, his face still and stern.

"Well, it might be a few months but…."

"Just tell me what your sentence is." Shakeem interrupted.

"18 months, is what the judge said," Shawn automatically started his manipulation, "But I figured I could get out in 12."

"No, that won't work." Shakeem said, thinking to himself.

"Well, I figured…" Shawn hesitated, "Never mind, you wouldn't be interested".

"Damn right I'm not." Shakeem turned without another word and walked to the other side of the square. Shawn was a little disappointed that Shakeem wasn't the least bit curious at his plan. He pretended not to care or notice, sticking to the notion that his idea would work.

At various places within the large square black lines demarcated portions of the area that were off limits. Just like in the treatment rooms, the ground opened much like the hydraulic cabinets in the walls of the room. Instead of a drawer or a box with items inside, there were televisions and chairs slowly rising from the ground. After the appliances and chairs were in place, the lines shifted again. The areas around the chairs were okay to use, the black lines dissipated, but the ones around the Televisions remained. No one was to touch them or else there will be consequences, the speakers reminded everyone. After this the screens flickered on, and each television was stationed to a different channel, a different genre. Some movies were on, mostly outdated things, and old television shows. Classics and some popular cartoons were on for the wide range of residents that might be enjoying free time at that moment.

Shakeem sat down on one chair facing a TV show featuring a cartoon cat chasing a cartoon mouse. The sound was low, but the subtitles were on. He mostly stared off into the distance, not quite thinking about or even considering what was going on in the episode, just wondering why the central computer would care about his behavior. If the consequences aren't the goal or even the main point of the program, then what was it? What exactly was he not showing to the computer that he started doing since the last time he was assessed? From the last treatment session to today he was apparently doing something different. It had only been a week, Shakeem thought. What had changed in a week? Shakeem looked around again, carefully this time. The lines on the ground were faded, but he could see the light fixtures just barely visible in the floor. He looked at the ceiling, noticing the vast array of cameras, their black dome-like heads still, quietly watching everything. He looked around at the pod doors, and then to the residents. The only thing he could think of was the new intakes.

What was he doing with the intakes that was better than before? Then he looked at Shawn.

Shawn was looking carefully, from a distance, at each television setup and then looked at the residents choosing to watch each type. Shakeem could tell what Shawn was doing; studying, making plans, trying to manipulate something or another. Shawn was a good con-artist, but his best feature is that people failed to notice him. With Shakeem watching him carefully, Shawn's behavior stood out.

Shawn made his way all the way around the square, careful not to step outside of the black line and just so happened to make his way to be seated next to Shakeem. Shakeem ignored him, or at least made it seem like it. Shawn smiled and laughed a little, "This is a good show, you have good taste man."

Shakeem shrugged, still thinking things through, but more aware of Shawn's purposes; Cautious, even.

"Look, dude. I'm just glad you helped me out the last week since I've been here it reall-"

"—Did you say for the last week?" Shakeem interrupted again.

"Could you just listen for a minute, I'm trying—"

"For the last week I've been helping you, doing what? Getting used to the program?" Shakeem answered his own question, and started to look to the ground again.

Shawn started talking, but Shakeem wasn't listening. His thoughts began to race. Was the way to get out of this place, and to avoid another extension merely to help another resident through their stay? He had kept to himself after his last extension, and even before then. After his initial bout

of consequences, and since his first chance to be released he had gotten into a fight, which of course resulted in a dangerous consequence of shocks, but also an extension for a few weeks. After that he shut down entirely until he met and started to follow Larry around. But the only thing since then that made him regain some social presence was helping this other resident. Is just helping another resident really the answer to all this? Shakeem wondered.

"So, it's not easy, but I know we can do it… if you'll help me" Shawn concluded.

"What the hell are you talking about?" Shakeem said, confused and a little annoyed.

"Well, that I'll help you out too if you need me to." Shawn said, smiling weakly. Playing pathetic might work on Shakeem, Shawn thought.

"Dude, just follow the instructions, it's not difficult." Shakeem said, still only half listening.

"Yeah, yeah, you know. But for the little things. The things they don't say." Shawn continued, lowering his head, attempting to seem weaker by folding his shoulders inward, and making himself seem smaller, timid.

"So, thank you."

"It's not difficult." Shakeem said, refusing to play Shawn's game.

Shawn stayed quiet, pretending to watch the show. Shawn wanted to do a few tests. He couldn't use himself, clearly, the risk of a consequence was high. However, if he could get enough people to step off the line, or break the same rule, perhaps he could cause an overload of data and that might make something happen. Shawn, at this point, merely wanted some questions answered.

Coeducational Programming

Paris wasn't always a boy's only school. There used to be girls, adults, and all sorts of people coming in and out of the building.

Tabitha found herself waiting for the others in line in the cafeteria. She heard the grinding of the vending machines shooting out wrapped packages of burgers, still warm from whatever was happening within the other side of the wall. She felt a sense of malaise as once again one of the machines were out of the main course and another machine booted up to take its place, lighting up and accepting orders from the residents as they stood in front of it. The male residents had already sat down for their meal and were eating on one side of the seating area within the black zone. Tabitha finally retrieved her food, and followed her orange line to the zone and cheerfully stepped over the line. She sat with her friends but within clear view of the boys at their tables. Shamelessly the boys flirted with the girls during the open area zone during meals, and shamelessly the girls pretended to notice and not notice simultaneously. Without being overly graphic, which the computer could easily detect and consequent, the residents developed their own codes fairly quickly.

"Aye Shawty, let me snart that bunk sometime?" One boy would say, referring to performing oral on a girl's backside.

"Only after you let me rock the banana boat until it crashes," another girl would say back, clearly referring to rough sex, or perhaps an act of oral sex.

The cafeteria would howl in laughter as the two groups found creative ways to sexually harass each other in the most obviously indirect way possible. The central computer was not able to keep up with the next words of slang, the differences in heat, or the changes in frontal or temporal lobe activity that would correspond in a limbic system shift that resulted in a clear concept of a curse word. As one would interpret a well-known swear word, there was a rough map of how one responds to hearing and one responds to saying it. The same pattern lights up for words used to replace those words, as long as the meaning is exactly the same. However, if the word is nonsense, or abstract, the added time of the signals become blurred. The word "banana" followed by "boat" looks nothing like "penis", "genitals", "dick", "cock" or any other phrase in the brain. For this reason, the computer converting and interpreting the resident's brain still couldn't read the resident's minds.

The programmers and psychologists watching the data were nervous that the algorithmic aspect of the A.I. would begin to confuse someone talking honestly about a banana boat, for whatever reason, would earn a shock after the computer learned that this could be a euphemism in another context. Tabitha was the first person to experience such a situation.

You see, the central computer, via the collars and the built-in sensors that measured neurochemical reactions and brain activity via the implant in each resident's brain sent signals giving brief images of what the resident was thinking about. General themes are selected based on the blueprint of what the brain is doing, cross referenced from intake screening of course, and then given to the computer to make judgements and assumptions about what the resident is intending to do. For example, Resident 103 often thought about violently stabbing his mother. Before he was sentenced to Paris, he was found stabbing a kitten in an alleyway. When he was admitted, his brain was scanned and prompted to think about stabbing, cats, kittens, his mother, danger, lust, blood, violence, running, and other factors that caused his brain to excite and light up in various ways. While Resident 103 walked through the hallways of the facility his brain would often recreate the same patterns of neural activity as it did when prompted in intake. 103 would be in the cafeteria line, and a resident might take too long: the omega pattern would resemble the same pattern of stabbing. 103 would wake up, but was still tired from a restless sleep, the pattern of blood or violence would appear. With the feedback from his adrenaline levels, his movement speed, and his brain pattern, the central computer could now *guess* when he was about to punch resident 244 in the back of the head in the bathroom, and administered a debilitating consequence, rather than a mild one for merely stepping off his colored line.

If the computer was only looking at his physical appearance, he could potentially still manage to punch another resident a few times, and have the other resident retaliate before immobilization. Fights at Paris were not permissible, and thus it was important to stop these behaviors full seconds before they occurred, not intervene during the action. The brain scans were helpful; however, they were not perfect. Not perfect at all when considering someone with an active imagination.

Tabitha sat in the cafeteria looking at one of the boys she often fantasized about at night time. She would often imagine his arms around her, his eyes looking at her, and their bodies intertwined in her bed at home. She would envision sitting with him in bed waiting for her mom to leave or look away and then the casually naughty things she would do to him and the sounds he would make when she touched him. She thought about servicing him orally, and him returning the favor at various places within the facility and outside in her previous life. But that day, in the cafeteria, she was thinking of some more aggressive sexual activities. Her crime involved many bloody and dangerous blunt force cases, and her intake assessment included many prompts that included sexual and violent images and scenarios. As she stood up to line up as the speakers told all residents to do, she was thinking briefly about how sexually appealing it would be to playfully fight with this boy and as he entered her, she would strangle him slightly. This image along with the arousal pattern made her limbic system overly excited. Her adrenaline increased along with other signature hormones and electrical signals that alerted the central computer to a potential of violence. Because of the rapid cycling of thoughts, and the increase of her brain activity to simulate rhythmic movement of her own body and that of another, the computer simply got confused.

From a computer's point of view, there is no difference between holding down a member of the opposite sex and penetrating with a knife or genitals if arousal is the result. Chasing down a deer and sinking in fangs releases endorphins, dopamine and serotonin just the same as chasing down a beautiful woman and having her smile and hand you her number for intended sexual intercourse later. The human mind elongates and truncates many experiences down to their biological origins, and beyond. A computer can only know what it is programmed to know. The extent of a robotic mind is the rules and scenarios given to it by an imperfect organic creator. Thus, Tabitha's punishment, for having a detailed sexual experience in her own mind, was that of a girl savagely jumping on top of a male resident, holding him down, and strangling him until climax. Such violence could not be tolerated, and thus the consequence was a few degrees less than lethal.

A few mistakes, yes. A problem here and there in the wiring, perhaps. But the chaos was interesting to say the least. Psychologists, engineers, computer scientists, and politicians had to agree that sex was too close to violence for a computer to reliably differentiate. Affection is the other side of obsession, and love was a fancy word for fear. In order to better reliably track one's sexual appetite in the abstract and one's violent nature in the physical less sexual stimuli must be present.

The solution: Segregation. For a while there were separate schedules. The male residents and female residents would be separated in schedule. Day time and night time schedules would be artificially created so there was minimal communication and minimal interaction between the two groups. However, this led to similar issues as minor to as major as Tabitha's. Eventually it was decided that the female population, which was smaller than the male population, should be exported. Eventually exactly that happened.

The facility was renamed, the algorithms were reimagined and better equipped to handle the boundaries of masculinity and the deviations. With one standard population, there are more specifications that could be added, and better codes used to better serve the population for rehabilitation. The Sapir School for Girls was up and running with a similar program, but similar specifications for girls. It was astonishing how much better both programs were once the genders were separated. All statistics increased in their benevolence, consequences decreased, and productivity increased overall. Distractions, are what the computer began labeling anything that caused progress to decrease and the organic minds agreed.

Shawn and Shakeem sat next to each other at dinner. It wasn't because Shakeem asked him to, or that he was even planning it. It just sort of happened. A lot of things just sort of happen when Shawn was around. Shakeem would walk through the hallway to his recreation time, and for some reason two residents would stage a fight within the black line. These two residents clearly weren't upset at each other. The swings they threw, the obvious distance they kept between each other, the loosely offensive language they spout at awkward moments, and seemingly attempting not to laugh. They were, of course, given a consequence that matched their aggression level, which was enough to make them sick, but not enough to knock them down. Shakeem noticed Shawn looking at the ceiling at the time, not the two boys squirm on the ground.

For some reason, three residents stepped off the line in unison before free time. They were given prompts to remain on the line, and the line became dashed and dotted to let the other residents know to stop. As the residents waited to be punished, Shawn was seen, again, looking at the walls, the floor, and the length of the hallway, not at the eventual wriggling boys on the ground.

These happenings were getting too common, and Shakeem was only mildly aware of them. When it just so happened that Shakeem found himself next to Shawn in line, and at the same table as himself, he knew to keep his guard up.

"It feels like a Thursday, you know?" said Shawn, more to himself than anyone else.

"It's Tuesday." Shakeem responded.

"Yeah, I thought so, but it just has that Thursday feeling… you know?" Shawn smiled.

Shakeem said nothing.

After a few moments of silence Shawn looked over Shakeem carefully. Shakeem's shirt wasn't wrinkly, he must fold his clothes when they're dispensed from the laundry. His shoes were basic, so he didn't spend a lot of energy on fashion or such. Shakeem was sitting, fairly aloof, slightly hunched, and slightly standoffish all at once. Shawn couldn't quite get a read on him; however, the other residents did seem to respect him. Shawn thought it might be better to try other sources. Maybe someone else would be useful and less complicated.

Shawn glanced around the room looking at the other candidates.

"Yeah, I thought so. You're wondering how the consequences work huh? Yeah. I know. Most people aren't interested in the complicated cyber-systems that observe and supervise. Do you know how much code is in that machine? Do you? It's fucking beautiful. Anyway, yeah, you'd love to try the simulator, wouldn't you? Haha. It's part of the interview process. Every administrator has to put it on as well as staff, whatever staff is left. Well, at least it used to be. Wouldn't it be good if police officers had to be arrested before they could be cops? Maybe lawyers forced to be litigated against or maybe put on trial before they could represent a client? Well, same logic. Don't worry they don't wear it for long. People in power don't want to feel pain. No one does. That's how it works, obviously.

"Nanobots, obviously. Yeah, 'Nanobots'. No, not thousands, not millions, but hundreds of millions. They swarm the nervous system of the brain; they get into the nerves of the body and they like to press against organs and whatnot. They do it automatically. It's just how they operate. These little bastards like to squeeze, and rip, and, also send back information and electric pulses, sure. That's the function really. It's just like your muscles. The default is to clench up. Ever see a stiff dead body? Ever try to move their arm? Imagine that dead fucker gripping your nut sack. Or his arm around your neck. Nanobots are programmed to do the same. Two little claws on each one, configured to swarm a specific place in the nervous system, and clench down. Chomp, chomp. Hahaha.

“So, there it is, nanobots just sitting there, swimming in the blood stream, squeezing, shocking, or ripping apart whatever they can. It hurts like a mother fucker, that’s for sure.

“So, you want specifics? Well, there are a few categories… Some bots go for the muscles for immobilization. Some go for the nerves to simulate heat or pressure. Hell, some, and these are for difficult clients, go straight for the thalamus. You know, number one switchboard. Mother board of sensation in the brain. Just one of those nanobots in your thalamus and you’ll swear someone chopped off your leg. Give a few hundred million of these suckers and you’ll swear your skin was being peeled off, slowly. …It isn’t inhumane! It’s… just how the bots operate.

“How do they end? Where do they go, you mean? Well, sure, a few will be inactive after a while. Even some might be peed out or shat out after a few turns in the stomach. Most of them will deactivate after nine months and just cease to function overall. Some bots, however, will actually help repair each other. But those are rarer, newer models. That’s all I know about the biology of it, I’m more part of the programming department, but it’s crazy right?

What?

What do you mean?

Well, obviously that’s what the collars are for. The signal to get them to stop stimulating.

"Without the collar, of course the nanobots would rip tissue and cells all the time. The collar is the only thing that stops those suckers. The collars are for safety. If you removed a collar, a resident would be ripped apart from the inside out." He wheezed. "It would just be a matter of time."

There were very few mirrors in the facility. Shawn wanted to see his collar a bit better, more detail, but he couldn't step off the line to reach closer to the mirror in the bathroom, nor could he use the reflective aspect of the glass in the cafeteria. He stood in the free time area square as the other residents were chatting and watching tv. He noticed another resident, a resident he recently took note of a few days ago after class. He didn't need to see his own collar; he could just view someone else's. He also didn't need to experience consequences himself to learn how this system worked, he just needed test subjects.

It was recently after class when Frank tripped. Without considering his future, he took the delay in consequence for a lack of attention on the part of whoever was monitoring the cameras. He stood up quickly, partially as a habit, and darted off the line down the hallway. He took around four steps before he collapsed and slid a full foot down the hallway. His arms and legs twitched violently as Shawn, still standing on the line, watching, looked over at him. The other residents remained quiet, some looking backward and around them to see what the commotion was, and others just simply ignoring the situation altogether. Frank, as the initial consequence subsided crawled toward the line as the warning and reminders sounded in his collar and overhead. He stood on the line again as the effects of the consequence waned entirely. Shawn nodded at him, in approval, rather than looking away in shame. Frank smiled and shrugged. "Worth a shot", Frank seemed to say. The line moved forward.

Frank sat on one of the couches, his arms folded. Shawn smiled, recognizing him as a hard headed person. He sat next to Frank in a casual way and faced the same direction. Frank, clearly affected by the change scooted over to give Shawn some space. Shawn turned to look at him sternly. "Hey, what's your problem anyway?"

"W-What?" Frank stammered, "I.. I didn't even do anything"

"Like, what the hell is wrong with you, running off the line like that and wasting all our time?" Shawn retorted as if the conversation had been started already. Frank smiled,

"Oh, that, yeah. Well…" he started to explain, in between rubbing his neck where the collar lay, "I just wanted to see if I could out run it, you know." He pointed upward. Shawn looked up and then back down. "Yeah, so what? The cameras? How do you outrun a camera?"

Frank laughed, "No no… think about it. It's a laser grid. When you step out of line the laser shoots your collar and the consequence starts. If you can outrun the laser, you can avoid consequences." He whispered and leaned a bit closer to Shawn, "you might even escape".

Shawn had to keep from laughing. Frank seemed to be more of an idiot than he realized. Shawn had to play the part, so he tried to look terrified. "You… You mean they're shooting lasers at us?" Shawn asked trying to sound genuine.

"That's right buddy. Think about it… why else would our collars have lights on them? You've played laser tag right? This whole place is just one big laser tag game… get it? Everyone on my pod is talking about it. We even have a plan to block the sensors so they can't shoot us!"

Shawn tried to seem amazed so he added a bit of fire to the theory, "Maybe that's why there are no mirrors…"

Frank looked puzzled, "Mirrors? I hadn't noticed." Frank thought Shawn was changing the subject entirely.

"You know," Shawn continued, "Mirrors.".

Frank laughed, "Dude, what does that have to do with anything?"

"Mirrors could be used to redirect the beam of light; the laser!" Shawn explained

"I'm not sure I understand what the hell you're talking about man." Frank looked around, partly trying to look for some context clues, and partly giving up on the conversation.

"If we grabbed a mirror, we could hold it up against our collar. When the laser goes to shoot the collar, the beam would be shot back at the camera, and we wouldn't get a consequence… right?"

Frank's eyes lit up, "OH! Exactly! See? It's got to be lasers! You get it!"

Shawn shook his head internally. He smirked outwardly and laughed a little, "Man, you're right… how are you going to get past the lasers without mirrors?"

Frank shook his head, "Not here. Too many people. We also think there are spies in here too".

Shawn smiled a little, curious at just how stupid Frank and his friends must be. "Really….? Spies?"

Frank was serious, and nodded looking around suspiciously. "Gotta be careful."

Frank stood up, looked around again, and walked away. Shawn smiled to himself. Maybe this would be easier than he thought.

Shawn heard the speakers begin, and everyone's collar began to light up. The lines on the cluster began to shine brightly and the residents quickly stood up to locate where they should be. All conversation stopped, and all motion continued without a second prompting.

The residents were split up now; some were heading to their pods to get changed for recreational activities, some to their scheduled treatment specialist appointments, and some for extra tutoring, given their program specifications. Today it was Shawn's turn to visit commissary. Shawn marched on the dark blue line out of the cluster doors and into the hallway. The residents were quiet but there was a friendly, even relaxed, tone in their steps. They did not lag behind or fail to step in tune with the line, but it was something about commissary that made them all feel human again. Shawn might have suggested that their collars were a bit easier to ignore on these days, and that the trip to commissary was nothing more than a group of friends heading to their corner store for some snacks. So far, Shawn had only visited the commissary room once. He had enough points for just one item, a poster for his room. It wasn't the sort of thing Shawn liked: some lush scene of ice and snow—something you'd see in a book of poems from an 11th grade creative English class. Shawn noted that the only available items to him were illuminated, and the other items were darkened out. Shawn only had twenty points that time, and he was curious to see how many he had earned since.

Since the enchanted days of psychological study and developmental progress in the realm of behavior, researchers have always found that positive reinforcement was essential to learning. A baby babbles and sputters sound and, of course, cries to receive what it wants. Soon, however, the baby's tastes are more subtle. Not only does the screaming crying baby want to be held, but held by auntie Sophia, not uncle Jackson. In order to convey these specific instructions, the baby has to adapt its continuous wailing into forming appropriate sounds. It makes the tedious sound of "Ah-Ah-Ah!", and suddenly the babe is pushed forward to Auntie. Soon there is a difference between being in Auntie's arms and being able to eat Auntie's freshly unwrapped chocolate chip cookie deluxe with added cream and sprinkles. In order for the baby to ask, successfully, for Auntie's freshly unwrapped chocolate chip cookie deluxe with added cream and sprinkles the child has to learn to differentiate between the sugar frosted ultra-whipped cream cookie with chocolate sprinkles. And thus, language is formed as the ultimate tool.

The power to define your reality and to label oneself is not to be scoffed at. Does a wolf know it is a wolf, or simply that it is not a tree, a cat, or a rock? While language exists in various forms it is always the one who speaks the language that can best define it as itself. Perhaps it's just a long-winded way of saying that only those who speak can know, and only those who listen can understand.

It's not difficult to see why positive reinforcement, getting what you want for doing something specific, is helpful and effective. Most people resent punishment or negative reinforcement. Having a negative stimulus being taken away if you do what needs to be done is nice and all, but you wonder why the stimuli was there to begin with. A baby cries and you give it a twenty-dollar bill, and then it shuts up. The baby cries again, applies the negative stimuli, and you give it a bribe to take away the negative mouth sounds. It's how humans work. Most robots don't work that way. No matter how much liquid nitrogen you give to a super conductor it merely performs the function programmed and capable. It cannot be bribed, not like a teenager. So, for teenagers the best way to convince them to continue to do an action is to reward them with things teenagers like: sex, risk, fun, food, and excitement. Those things teenagers will fight for, kill for, and die for. It doesn't make much sense, though, unless we look deeper than psychology, into neuroscience.

It's the classic neuroscience study linking brain and behavior. We gave a mouse the option of two buttons. One button opened a hatch and gave the mouse one food pellet and the other button was attached to an electrode surgically implanted into the mouse's brain. The electrode directly stimulated the area of the brain correlated to the sensation and pleasure of eating. The mouse was exposed to one button at first, just merely eating one pellet at a time. It was a happy mouse. It would explore the cage, sniff the air, examine the walls, but eventually get hungry, or perhaps bored, and sniff the button, press it, and eat for a while. But this is merely feeding a pet, the experimental question was: If we give the mouse a choice of pure bliss compared to the mediocre elements of existence, which would the mouse choose? Instead of just merely eating a single pellet of food with each press we induce the pure bliss of nourishment, the second button. The mouse switched from pressing the button that gave it actual food, to the button that stimulated its brain into thinking it received food, maybe even the best version of food. Maybe it was a bit hedonistic, and a bit selfish, sure, but the true understanding of this experiment is that the mouse wasn't able to understand its own brain. All it could do was feel good and full and move its little paws. Obviously, the mouse starved to death, still pressing that lever with all its heart. It doesn't make much sense, though, unless we look deeper than neuroscience, into philosophy.

Was the pleasure worth starving to death?

Only the mouse would know.

Human beings spend a lot of time chasing after items that can stimulate that feeling of nourishment in the brain. So many times, we have people pressing a button at work, or pressing a button in a relationship, or a lever in their children, in a slot machine, in alcohol, or drugs, or sex, or risk, or excitement, or food, or fun. It's interesting to see what a human will get sick of, even if it is nothing but pleasurable. At what point do the cells in the brain finally give up as the chemicals devour themselves for working too well? There was a school that tested that very same idea, but in reverse.

We already knew that positive reinforcement was easy. You could make a resident stab himself in the eye with a rusty knife if you stimulated the right part of the brain in the right sequence, and I don't mean controlling his arms and hands. With enough endorphins, oxytocin, dopamine, and the right neuro-structures, you can probably convince a person to tear their own heart out and eat it if paired with the right positive sensations. If people can ruin their marriages and traumatize their families for the thrill of an orgasm through the conduit of an affair, just how much would they destroy if you offered them those sensations directly into their own skulls?

However, at what point does a person just let the baby cry? How long do you stand in the rain before you open your umbrella? When does a person succumb to the overwhelming power of negative reinforcement? Human beings are much more complicated than a mere lab mouse, and they are able to experience many different positive and negative sensations, both of which could bring about pleasure or pain, and combinations of each. There is a poetic aspect to the nature of mankind, and suffering appears to be the rhythm of it all. These elements could be tested. Of course, creating a situation to explore what mixture of sensations were needed to coax a test subject into harming itself in order to be relieved of pain would be ironic and could possibly create psychological madness, but madness and irony researchers were not interested in. If being a good member of society was the target behavior, what could be offered in exchange? One might think an excess of pleasure, but others considered a brief, yet powerful, injection of pain instead. It doesn't make much sense, though, unless we look deeper than philosophy, into experimentation, and that should be easy, if you have a never-ending supply of test subjects and of course, a private facility.

There were only a few tours every few years open to anyone, and the press was rarely, if ever, invited. Most of the time these tours were highly contested over an incident or a press conference that occurred earlier on in the year. During these 'Town Hall' meetings, many of the people invited to speak on behalf of the Paris program were politicians or lobbyists quick to show off the statistical data; the extremely low recidivism rate, the lack of escape, the lack of crime, and slight increase in taxes compared to the overwhelming increase in property value. Short and sweet phrases made the headlines of the papers, "No crime, for only a dime", "It's worth it when we work less", "Monitoring done well!", etc. Seldomly questions were answered in these meetings that weren't already pointed in a favorable light, there was some pomp and circumstance to suggest other questions could be answered as well.

Such a meeting was scheduled, and the Town Hall room was packed with people with questions. This meeting was supposed to be about the merger of city and public files into a private facility's processing computational and storage programs. After the general town hall meeting there would be a tour for those invited. Who, exactly, was on the invitation list no one knew for sure; the list was selected with help from the central processor, and could be updated at any time.

Ally sat in one of the rows designated for journalists and slowly, and sadly looked around. The crowd behind her were young children and mothers, some clutching handkerchiefs and framed pictures of loved ones, probably those hurt or lost because of Paris. Ally thought it looked more like a memorial service than a press conference, and felt that the entire mood of the room was grim. She tried not to look around anymore but there would be a shout of turmoil in the audience occasionally. "What the hell is taking so long!" someone would shout behind her, and she would turn around, startled. "Fuck Paris!" someone else might yell, and there would be noisy murmuring from the crowd before security would usher them out. Even the other journalists next to her seemed determined and quiet. Typically, the journalism pit would be filled with talks of new leads and perhaps how an interview went the day or weeks before. Sometimes there would be some gossip or an interesting story in the works. Sometimes they would even go over certain points each journalist wanted to go over as they would work together and coordinate to maximize their time in getting answers. However, today they were quiet, sitting still, facing forward, as if being watched. There were only 3 journalist spots on the roster for the tour, and each of the twelve of them wanted it.

As with most things, the meeting started a few minutes late. And with most things there were last minute changes. The panel for the conference was supposed to be two or three random speakers picked from the Division of Justice & Corrections along with a psychiatrist. There was an addition to the group which was labeled A.I.L.. Ally took note of this in her pamphlet, and even broke the nervous silence to ask the peer to her side. No one knew, of course, and so they merely waited until the meeting began. All at once the politicians and doctors arrived, walked up the stairs to the raised platform and took their seats at the table covered in white cloth behind their respective name placards. Then, a man in a white lab coat walked in with a briefcase. He set it on the table behind the A.I.L placard and flipped it open. The audience was quietly watching this as it occurred, as the other panelists took note of their expressions. Suddenly radio feedback blared through the speaker system. As everyone winced and shriveled at the sudden ear-piercing screech, Ally took note to keep watching the briefcase. The sound dissipated, and the man in the white coat walked away. The briefcase was sitting open, the top half facing the audience. It was an odd-looking briefcase with a black metallic finish along with reinforced steel holding the seams together along the hinges, however there was a large camera lens embedded in the surface. It glowed a bright blue and seemed to move quickly from each face in the room. Suddenly the speakers crackled once more.

"I apologize for the sonic feedback. I hope it woke some of you up", a soft masculine voice stated. "I also apologize for the delay, there were some complications in my delivery to this stage. Let me introduce the panel, and then myself, and then we can begin."

The audience was quiet, but this wasn't the first them they had been spoken to by a robotic A.I. Most of their mobile devices had this feature, along with the occasional companion robot or public service depot. Automation was everywhere. This was, however, one of the first times the audience had seen this technology in its raw form. There were no sleek human-esque features. No added cheek bones, or cute smiles painted onto lifeless cold metal bodies. Just a bulky case, an eye, and a voice. This was unlike a vending machine or the automated transport systems, this object seemed to be able to think. Some felt intimidated.

"We have with us, today, the Vice Chairman of Public Defense, the Secretary of Corrections for this district, Dr. Chanel and Dr. Amir, leaders of the Paris Program, and myself, the Artificial Intelligence Liaison to facilitate discussion and lead the tour of the facility." After a few moments of silence, the bright blue glow dissipated into a quiet pulse, and the Secretary of Corrections, in his basic black suit, white shirt and black tie, began to speak.

"We're seeing basically all the same data from last time. Our sector's crime rate is 50% lower than the lowest sector's rate since the year 2020, and even after you factor in changes in laws and subsequent shift in prices, crime has been falling at a rate of 2% each cycle….." he continued in his gruff matter of fact voice. He spoke as if he had just explained this information a few moments ago and was solely touching on the talking points, the raw conclusions. No one cared, however. They were still looking at the sentient briefcase.

"Thank you, Secretary," the AIL stated as his blue light lit up again. "Does anyone have questions for the Secretary of Corrections?" The light dimmed slowly, as if to give the audience permission to speak. After a few moments of silence, the voice from the speakers continued, "Very well, next is Dr. Chanel. What do you have for us, doctor?"

Dr. Chanel stood up and put both of her fists down on the clothed table and stared at the crowd in a stern manner. She looked over the crowd from one side and then the other allowing her white lab coat to drape slightly over the table. Then, in a thick, what seemed to be German accent, she said, "Ve haffe created zee himbosible here! Look at just ein example of zee technology ve haffe achieved. Vile zee process might not be entirely for zee meek of heart, vith zis technology ve can reffolusionise zee vorld. Ve can change how people exhist, live zeir lives, defend zemselves, und make normal decisions! Zis is zee future!" She immediately sat down and folded her arms. She then stated after a moment, "No Questions!"

AIL started glowing a bit brighter again, "Okay. Thank you Dr. Chanel." After a few moments of silence AIL started to speak again, "Next we have the Vice Chairman of Public Defense".

The secretary stood up from his seat in his green suit decorated with war medals and awards. He stood with a grim look on his face as well, and looked into the crowd. In a soft, deep, tone he began. "I know a lot of you have lost loved ones in this process. And I know many of you believe the system is unjust. People have died in order to create balance and order, and I am saddened to see those that have lost someone dear to them. To the mothers and siblings in the audience that have lost their sons and brothers to the Paris Program, I am truly sorry for your sacrifice. And I understand that this is worse than war. Your sons did not sign up to die, but instead to be given another chance. What they found instead was error, human and robotic. I am saddened to look at the numbers here, and understanding what true sacrifice looks like." He paused for a moment, his eyes growing glassy as he looked down. Ally heard a few people behind her sniffle, and someone quietly sob.

Dr. Chanel stood up suddenly and slammed her fist down on the table once more, "Nein! This is not zee moment for tears!" she pointed at the audience with a fist and then extended her index finger, "Through zacrifice ve are crafting ein new vorld! It is not time to be zad or throw zee pain out! Ve must ko vurther vith our hexperimentation und deeben zee holds of our hintellect on our ovn nature. Vith each moment ve are kathering more data und effery zing ve haffe vorked zo hard for ve still continue to zeek out und heffentually conquer!" She again sat down in a huff, and glared at the Vice Chairman, who was still standing.

"I must agree with the doctor," The Vice Chairman said slowly, still holding back tears, "You remember how it was just a few years ago. Before this system was in place, and with the rise of automation, young boys had little to hope for. Basic high school jobs were automated, and our youth resorted to crime and other unscrupulous activities to pass the time and to make something of themselves. Without minimum jobs, those who didn't immediately get a grasp on school work became demoralized. Instead of learning discipline and striving for an education, many of them chose to go down dark and dangerous pathways. But, because of this program we can try to save our youth and this next generation. While it's true we have gone far and have asked you all to sacrifice for the good of the district, we also must continue. We cannot stop. I hope you all can understand what we are trying to get done here. Thank you." He sat down and wiped his eyes quietly, as Dr. Chanel rolled her eyes.

"Thank you Vice Chairman," AIL said as his lights returned to normal. Are there any questions for the panel so far? Most of the crowd murmured to each other, but no one wanted to start a shouting match with Dr. Chanel, or risk being ejected from the conference by security for asking a bad question. For those who were angry with Paris, they just received an apology, and for those who were curious, they wanted to go on the tour, not asking questions they knew most of the answers to already. Each of them wanted to see the facility, and none of them would be able to if they were unruly or posed a security risk. Even as the few deeply, personally affected, clutched the photos of their dead kin, they knew they had to remain civil. It was the only way, for Ally at least, to earn closure.

It was nearly a month since Shawn was admitted, and still he seemed to only have the bare minimum in commissary tokens. While the others stepped up to the larger monitor, placed their finger on the fingerprint scanner, stated their ID number into the voice recognition box, and waited for the points to be calculated, it was clear that Shawn was still not going to earn nearly enough for anything extravagant. Shawn still didn't quite know how to earn them either. Some residents could afford an extended recreation pass or even luxury items in the cafeteria. Two residents even bought themselves a large chocolate cake slice, something that most residents haven't had in months or even years. Each resident wanted something, not for the sake of value, but for the sake of novelty. Certain items were able to be fastened to the wall to decorate their room walls. Some could purchase little toys or even a small ball to bounce during their time in their rooms. Residents were not allowed to play with their items during movement or during an activity, but in their rooms, they were fully capable.

Shawn looked nervously as the line moved down. The Commissary room was fairly small. Just enough for a line of residents at a time to go up to the large screen and back around toward the exit. "Please step forward and place your finger on the touch screen", the overhead speaker would say as the next resident stepped up. "Please state your ID number now", it would say after the fingerprint scanner displayed the number. "Your total is 3,221 points for your behavior. You may spend 3,221 points at this time. Please select your items", the speaker would say to the resident a few places in front of Shawn. The resident took some time deciding. He looked over the buttons on the screen ranging from a notebook to a portable music player. He could only afford moderate items, nothing too expensive or extravagant, but still nice enough. With a shaky finger, and with everyone watching behind him, he selected a poster of a pop star, and a nicer pillow. The screen lit up around these items and his points were deducted before his eyes. "Your new balance is 121 points. Please step aside," the speaker stated, as the screen went dark. The resident shuffled along. The next resident stepped up, and followed the directions. The speaker stated that he had 700 points to spend. He selected one of the only few items on the screen, some styled pencils, and his points went down to 200.

It wasn't clear exactly how each point was tabulated; some would suggest that it was based on adherence to the rules and norms. Shawn knew that not every rule was followed exactly. One could place their foot deliberately a few centimeters off the line and there would be no consequence. Shawn tried to figure out if, perhaps, there was some trigonometric function between the angle of the guideline and the position of one's foot to determine whether a resident was stepping off the line purposefully, or if they were merely walking with poor posture. However, perhaps these minor differences were the elements that led to earning points with each step or remaining destitute. Shawn didn't quite have the timing to test this, seeing as commissary wasn't a routine thing. Only after some time would commissary be granted and not for every resident each time. It would be difficult to see immediately if one action led to an increase of points if another action led to a deduction of points, there were simply too many variables to consider. Shawn wasn't sure where he would be on the spectrum. He placed his finger on the fingerprint scanner, and stated his number aloud. The monitor flickered for a moment and then his score was present.

"Zero? Seriously? Zero?" Shawn said loudly in line. "There's been a mistake, I ---", Shawn felt the sharp pains in his sides as they traveled inward toward his heart. He clutched himself tight and fell to the ground. "Please no talking in the line", a localized voice stated from his collar. Suddenly the pain was gone. His chest relaxed and his nerves responded as normal. There was no more pain, but what he was feeling was anger. He trembled, trying to keep himself together as he stood up. He turned around on the line to see his peers looking, and purposefully not looking, at him. He bowed his head and followed the line away from the computer. His mind was racing. "This is some joke then," he thought. "They wanted me to see this, that I had no points, they wanted me to see that I wasn't earning anything. Those bastards." Shawn thought furiously to himself as he looked at the ground. They don't invite people to commissary for their own sake, he thought, they just do it to make a mockery out of people. They do it to establish some control, some internal conflict. It's their own little social experiment, I bet. Those bastards! He cursed them in his head.

He continued to process the situation when he noticed an average pair of shoes walk by. He instantly recognized them as Shakeem's. Shawn lifted his head up now, and watched the line form behind him as resident after resident selected their items to be delivered to their rooms later. Shawn noticed the extra cabinet drawer in his room that would not open. One morning he asked a question to his personal babysitter, the camera on the wall. "What is that second drawer for?" Almost instantly a prerecorded voice started to answer a general questions about room accommodations.

“In your room you will find one desk, one chair, windows, one bed, two drawers, one for your daily outfit, and one for your commissary items to be dispensed and disposed of. Your clothes will be extracted and cleaned at the facility’s discretion and returned back to you before you need them again. If you have any further questions please press the button and speak into the microphone. Thank you!”. Shawn asked a few more questions that were more specific and varied. However, the monitor merely recorded his question and flickered on and off. No answers that day. Today, however, he watched Shakeem, wondering what item would arrive in his cabinet this evening. What sort of thing would Shakeem want? If he had a lot of points, maybe a guitar? If only a few, perhaps a deck of cards. Somewhere in the middle, perhaps an extra snack, or a drink of some sort. Shawn’s imagination went wild at the possibilities.

Shakeem stepped up to the computer, and with a shrug placed his finger down on the scanner. Shakeem mumbled his number, and the screen displayed his points. “Your total is 40,903,261 points for your behavior. You may spend 40,903,261 points at this time. Please select your items”, the speaker stated. Many of the residents murmured, and looked around at each other, none making more than a whisper of a sound. Shawn couldn’t believe it.

Shakeem looked at the items and then took a step away from the screen. He selected nothing, and lined up behind the others waiting in line. No one moved for a few moments, many just watching him reject the thousands of options lighting up on the screen. Some strained to see what sort of prizes he had access to, things that most residents have never seen appear on their option screens. Some residents just stared at Shakeem. As he walked away and stopped at the end of the line, he shrugged his shoulders, and stood still. The next resident stepped up to the screen, and for a brief moment felt that he could select any item available. The screen immediately went to black, and the prompt started over again. “Please step forward and place your finger on the touch screen”. The line continued in silence.

“I will be showing you around the facility myself,” stated Dr. Amir, as the conference concluded. Ally finished writing her notes along with the other journalists, and they sat up straight as the names would be announced. “Before we go, however, I want to express how important it is what we are trying to do. All of our speakers today have touched on interesting and helpful points, but it isn’t just the sake of science, or the sake of sacrifice. I want to be clear that this technology is primarily used for rehabilitation. Your children,” he stopped and pointed at the crowd in a gentle manner, his fingers extended outward as if offering them a seat, “are the focus here. You as parents, loved ones, guardians of their futures, have entrusted your progeny to us. We in return have made a promise to perfect and format this process for the future and for the present. Mistakes can be made, but with risk comes progress.” Dr. Amir stopped speaking to look at the crowd. He then looked at the panel and gave them all nods. Once they nodded back, Dr. Amir beaconed to the two in white lab coats to come and attend to AIL. AIL seemed to sit quietly his bright blue light fairly dim, still analyzing the faces in the crowd. The others in the panel stood up and walked off the stage in single file. Dr. Amir, AIL and their workers remained. The audience began to murmur.

Ally sat impatiently, looking at Dr. Amir and the attendants meddle with the briefcase. She couldn’t tell what they were doing with it, but she wanted to say at least something. She stood up and cleared her throat. Dr. Amir barely noticed her as he was preoccupied with AIL. Ally raised her hand now, started to sweat with anxiety. A colleague next to her whispered for her to sit down. Ally waved her hand back and forth, and muttered, “Ex-Excuse me?” with an upward inflection. Dr. Amir still failed to notice.

Suddenly, the speakers crackled once more and AIL’s blue light shined brighter. The attendants stopped working for a moment and looked for a reason for A.I.L. to suddenly change. “Ms. Aaliyah Shakeem, do you have a question for the panel?” The audience grew silent again. Dr. Amir squinted at the crowd looking for the one AIL mentioned. He focused on a brown-skinned woman, average height and weight with black hair resting at her shoulders. Her pantsuit outfit fit her snuggly. Ally, as her brother called her, stood with her notepad and pen and found that her mouth was drying up. She cleared her throat again, swallowed, and started, “Not to be rude, but I was hoping to see the facility today. Is there any way that can happen?” The journalists seemed stunned. The crowd seemed stunned. Some whispers in the back of the room traveled across the aisles and Dr. Amir sighed. He looked at the attendants and they looked back at him. “That…” Dr. Amir stated, “That is up to our liaison.” He then pointed with his fingers to A.I.L. Ally looked expectantly from Dr. Amir to AIL, as the speakers started to hum. “Ms. Shakeem, you are on our list to depart directly after this meeting. Along with Ms. Shakeem are Mr. and Mrs. Cuff, Dr. Beruka, Ms. Sheedy, Mr. Byron…..” the voice of AIL continued on. Ally sat back down in her chair, feeling a bit light headed. The stress of those very few moments were enough to make her faint. She, however, knew she couldn’t afford to show weakness now. She was on the list, perhaps since the beginning, but she dared not to put too much of a spotlight on herself, especially after that stunt. No one knew what factors determined an invitation, so everyone decided to stay as close to the norm as possible. This was a helpful strategy, as being disqualified seemed to be an easier feat than randomly possessing qualifications.

As the list concluded, AIL invited those on the list to one of the doors near the front of the room behind the stage. He asked the others to leave. Many voices rang out, some screaming obscenities, others threatening the doctors and AIL themselves. Some attempted to throw objects at the stage, as security quickly rushed these individuals. Carefully and without being too noticeable those whose names were called briskly made their way through the crowd of people and toward the front door. Ally nodded to her journalism colleagues that were allowed in, and gave a sympathetic frown to those who were not invited. Ally made her way across the aisle and around groups of frustrated guests who wanted to be invited to the tour. She looked at the sea of faces once more, seeing disgust, pain, hopelessness, and curiosity, in almost everyone. She knew the anger she felt inside of her, and knew how the parents of lost ones, incarcerated ones, and dead ones felt. She was determined, at the very least if not for her sake, for theirs, to find her brother; her brother, and answers.

Part 2

The security drones flew overhead. Ally counted four around AIL once it exited the building in the arms of the mechanics responsible. Dr. Amir was busy looking at new data on his data pad while security personnel waited by the parking lot. Four auto-vans arrived in black with tinted windows. Dr. Amir, seemed to wonder off while the security detail gave orders. Each had a list in their hand and they read off names while directing individuals to their assigned vehicles. Ally would be in car number 3. As the tour guests organized themselves, Ally saw the drones leave the proximity of the briefcase and instead hover above the cars silent, one for each van. One guest asked the security officer what the drones were for. "For our protection and yours". Not satisfied, the guest began to pry. "Your protection? From who? From what?"

"In the event of an unruly guest," he lingered on the word 'guest', "…the drone, armed with a series of injectable capsules from stun to lethal will engage. Don't be a problem".

"Wait, I didn't sign up to be injected with anything. I didn't sign anything; this is ridiculous" the guest stated pompously. The other guests that could hear murmured quietly.

The security guard looked at his list, "You are Dr. Elijah?"

"Yes, yes I am, and I know my rights."

The guard made a quick swipe on his electronic pad. "Please step out of line"

"Wh-What? I was invited by Dr. Amir himself. I will not leave."

The drone atop car two turned and faced the Dr. Elijah. The security officer stood perfectly still. The other guests in line started to back away slowly from the guest, Dr Amir looked up briefly, then back to his data.

"L-Look, I'm sorry. Let's just go." Dr. Elijah stammered.

"Please step out of line, this is the final directive." The security guard stated without blinking.

Dr. Elijah took a few steps out of line, still looking at the drone that was tracking his movements.

Ally noticed that there was no one controlling the drone, none that she could see anyhow. She wondered how the drone knew who to target and for how long. The drone, after Dr. Elijah left the line and returned to the building, return to its position atop the car. Without moving the security guard waved on the next guest and the line continued. So many questions, questions that she as the media should be able to ask, however she knew her questions would be monitored and studied before answered. The wrong step, the wrong word, or the wrong inflection could change everything. She stepped into the car and found her seat.

Shakeem stood on the deck of the boat as the waves pushed it from side to side. He stumbled and stabled himself, and unsheathed his sword. Staring down the shaft of the sword, he charged forward at the pirate in front of him, spinning around to clash against another pirate's sword. A flash of light distracted him and a robotic octagon with a red eye floated by. His sister's voice told him to be calm, but he felt more upset than ever. He looked down and found himself in a tube, filling with warm liquid. Another flash of light, and he was alone now, in his bedroom, still holding his bloody sword. He asked himself out loud, "Who did I kill?".

Shakeem woke up in his cell, a few minutes before the chimes and prompts would begin. The automated voice started to say the necessary prompts for those awakening too early. As one does, Shakeem checked quickly around his room for his sword, and shook off the lurking sensation of his impending doom from drowning and any sources of water, perhaps under his bed, or in the corner of his room. After a few seconds, though, like the consequences, these feelings were gone.

Ally slid her panties back on, one leg at a time. Crouching by the bed in the hotel room, the cheap wooden boards creaked as the security defense councilman snored rhythmically. She moved silently toward the window, smoothing out her dress and tucking her bra into her purse. No reason to be proper at this point, she thought to herself as a dirty feeling continued to wash over her, his seed still inside. She glanced at the overcast sky, the darkened gray light shining through the window on the Tuesday afternoon. Ally held herself tight, partly for the cold, and partly for the warmth. And partly to tell herself that she was one step closer to getting into the press box for a town hall meeting where a certain machine would pick her out of the crowd for a tour. Her purse contained a press pass, won over dinner, kissing, and faux passionate love-making with a man who made decisions. She thought the trade was worth it, worth it just for a chance.

The councilman stirred and her thoughts were disrupted. She went to the bathroom to straighten herself, and came out feeling a little better. The warm water, and the freshly applied makeup was enough to make her feel a bit like herself on the outside, even if it was a version of herself beyond the original. When she returned home, she would take a full shower and reorient herself to her real goals.

Walking down the street, she hailed the first public auto car she could reach. Her wrist band only authorized her for class C and below vehicles, but the press badge allowed her access to B vehicles, which were much roomier. When she programmed the car and it dropped her off at her dwelling complex, she felt the sweat and shame of her actions build up again, and bubble into her cheeks as heat settled onto her neck and head. By the time she entered the elevator to her apartment, reached her door, used her key to unlock it, and lock it behind her, opened the blinds with a flick of her wrist, turned the heater on with a snap and the news on, she was sobbing. She sunk into her kitchen chair and cried, holding her press badge in one hand, and her own arm in the other. This would be easy, she thought, this would blow over. She took off her wrist band and started to disrobe. The television broadcasted the centralized news station, which currently had coverage of the huge line to gain qualification into the town hall meeting that would be taking place in two days. The sound was off, and Ally wasn't paying attention. Through sniffles and sobs, she went to the shower and rinsed and scrubbed his sweat and semen off and out of her. This would be the last time she would have to do anything like that, she told herself. The steam from the shower rested and condensed on a picture frame holding two happy dark-skinned teenagers looking up at the sun miles away from her, both of which were gone now.

"It's part of the contract, you know. I didn't decide to do it. This thing has a mind of its own it seems. The local governmental oversite has little to do now but sit back and judge the system based on the statistics the very same system conjures up. It's almost madness. How do you check the math of a super computer that is more powerful and accurate than any other computer? How do you avoid spending the rest of your life trying to recheck a single data point this monster created in a 20th of a second? Politicians don't understand the science, just polls. And the polls say there should be some public transparency. The central processing units in these facilities insist on isolation from the public in order to maximize results and it just so happens that results poll fairly high. No politician wants to be the one who pulled the plug on a system that reduces crime, even if, for exchange, a few bodies show up, but you know all about that.

"Being a Paris Resident can be placed on a resume, and in many cases these previous residents get first pick with jobs and opportunities, even schools and scholarships due to the known success of the program. No resident goes through the system twice, and no previous resident ever regresses back into crime. Not a single one.

"Those results you couldn't even ask a higher power for. And there wasn't one to ask that could calculate human behavior as well as the central computer at a facility like Paris Correctional." He wheezed again, taking a sip of his water.

Shawn sat in class absentmindedly. He had some data now, some pieces of the puzzle. His eyes glazed over as the sound of the recorded teacher droned on and on. The class seemed rigid, the air seemed stale and the entire room seemed to be made of a hardened clay to Shawn. He could mold it if he really tried, much as he had acted in the real world. While he was young, he knew that lying was merely a tool, and manipulation was mankind's contribution to the stale universe. Others, however, saw it as just another dumb kid being a jerk.

There was a delay, Shawn thought, between the shocks and the transgression. About half a second. He thought about this as images of his peers danced into his brain. He convinced one resident to step off the line just before lunch and one just after, the hypothesis being that the task of lunch distribution might delay the circuits. No significant findings. He thought that perhaps the shocks would be faster after treatment time, since there was an option for the cameras to go off now and then, he heard, and thus more power to the cameras after reactivated. This was not the case either. He convinced a few peers to fake fights during the free time area in order to see what the master computer would do and how long it would take to completely immobilize someone who had the intent, or the motivation, to cause bodily harm. Sadly, the other residents were terrible actors, and the shocks never seemed to rise above a warning in those cases. Shawn had to witness and study a real fight.

Bernie woke up to the sound of his alarm, or more accurately, the sound of his own yelling after his wrist alarm shocked him; a novelty for heavy sleepers. The overweight man slumped over his bed and sloppily put on his slippers, heaved a big sigh, along with a long wheeze, and stood up to use the bathroom. Mold grew between the cracks of the tile, and the cracked mirror showed a cramped bathroom with clothes and opened bottles of lotion, shampoo, and toothpaste tubes littered around the sink. In the center of the split image from the mirror was Bernie: middle aged, hunched over, distinctly and constantly wheezing, and eyes half closed, ready for another two-week shift at Paris Youth Correctional Facility.

Bernie adorned the basic outfit, one of the seven clothing combinations all employees must wear under their worker jumpsuit. His outfit for the next two weeks would be comprised of a t-shift and basic shorts. No pockets, and no images or lettering. Just the clothing. He sluggishly wandered to his table and spoke into his voice-automated fridge what he would like for breakfast, the last breakfast of a free man. "Toast and eggs", he said blankly with a heave for air after the statement that ended in a distinguished wheeze. He sat at the table as his oven and toaster began pre-heating and the mechanical arm attached to the refrigerator gathered the ingredients. Bernie's eyes slowly closed as he wheezed himself to sleep at the living room breakfast counter, the only place in his apartment where the mechanical arm could reach, and began to snore. After around 12 minutes the clatter of a plate dropping in front of him woke him up. After a grunt of surprise, he saw his toast and eggs settled on the plate in front of him, perfectly cooked and presented with a few strawberries. "Thank you," Bernie said loud enough for the refrigerator's microphone to hear him. The mechanical arm retracted into its slot within the refrigerator door. The oven and toaster turned off, and the room was silent, all but for the chomping, chewing, and wheezing of Bernie.

Bernie took the lift down to the underground parking section attached to his apartment. He was able to afford a fairly nice auto-ride and a fairly nice parking place, although he did not go out as much as one would expect. Bernie used his haptic password and entered the vehicle seat. The seats connected into a semi-circle, and the mid-section was hallowed out to make room for the touch screen and voice interface. Because there was no steering wheel, the rider only had to choose a location and let the vehicle find the best route based on previous suggestions, or current inputs. Bernie was barely awake, and let the vehicle make up its own mind. The auto-ride began to turn up the heat, as previously indicated as favorable, and a smooth jazz radio station, which Bernie barked, “Off!” to. The auto-ride became quiet as the engine started up and began to roll fluidly across the ground and into traffic. If Bernie was awake, he’d see the people of the city gawk and awe at such a sophisticated auto-ride travel by. He would have noticed a few people reaching out to touch the sleek surface and the one-way mirrored windows that showed the passersby their own shocked and inquisitive faces. Only celebrities and very rich people could afford such a machine, and most of those people do not live in a city like this. Bernie’s unconscious body passed by a few back roads and a few highways maintaining an average speed of the cars around him, or the suggested speed of the road when no other vehicles were present, all while being nestled in the comfort and luxury of his auto-ride.

There was a familiar “clunk”, and Bernie shook himself awake. “AutoRide Disengaged, External Guidance Activated, To Request Override, press or state Override”, the auto-ride chirped. Bernie said nothing. He looked out the window to see that he had arrived at the outer gate of the facility, and the parking lot computer had disengaged his auto-ride. The parking computer would guide his vehicle the rest of the way. To the guard tower computer, it meant there was one more person to account for in the maximum population roster, and one more person to fire upon if certain exit procedures were not met. To the Central computer of Paris, there was going to be another data point to add to the array of information to consider, process, and monitor. To Bernie, that meant he could sleep for another seven minutes until they reached the central gate that led into the employee parking lot at a grueling 10 miles per hour.

Bernie arrived at the dedicated spot, and the doors unlatched and opened. He stepped out by the few other cars parked along the parking lot and took a walk toward the first guarded pathway. Bernie looked out along the fields that seemed to never end between one fence and the other. He smiled at the idea of some dumb kid getting to this point and not being able to fathom how painful the bullet darts would be as they rained down on the kid’s body. In a secondary sense, Bernie scanned for weaknesses along the fence, more so out of his training than for his concern. He also noticed some of the automatic sentry guns, diagonally rotating their muzzles, constantly looking for an excuse to fire a debilitating or lethal round. He waddled past the first station waving his identification badge. The guard waved him in. He continued into the corridor as the large double steel doors opened and he was greeted by another armed guard station. This station required computerized biometric scans, so he had to stand still while the computer cleared him. Bernie didn't mind, he was impressed by the system itself. He thought about the cost of such a machine to be running consistently throughout the building. If Bernie's behaviors, or biometrics strayed significantly, he would know in the control room. As Bernie's markers were outlined, and his identity was processed, a unique badge was created for his usage, for the next two weeks at least, and a line on the ground started to glow yellow. His badge started to glow yellow as well, and he placed the badge around his neck. The armed guards waved him inside. Once he entered the steel doors closed behind him as the sally port opened in front of him. For just a moment there was a light that shone between the outside and the inside of the building. Bernie was not happy with that and made a mental note to speed up the door locking mechanism on this entry point. He walked through, vaguely following the yellow line. He knew where it led, and he knew what it was designed for. He designed it himself just for his biometrics. He moved around the external facility, shaped like a square around the correctional facility and looked through the large glass-paned windows. He observed the large gray solid block of a building sitting on the grassy plane in front of him. "There they are, my children," he said to himself tapping on the glass as if it were a fish bowl.

Bernie walked through the double doors of his office and sat in his chair. The other programmer sat there in silence as he closed up some programs on one of the computers he was working on. Bernie's station, however was already dark. The multiple monitors and consoles were not on for the last two weeks. The other programmer started to power his station down, a similar, but smaller console, and stood up to leave.

“Hey wait, jackass, aren’t you forgetting something?”, Bernie said to the other programmer.

“Look, I know you don’t care Mr. Douglas, but my name is Wendell.”, the programmer responded.

“Hey, Jackass, why don’t you clean up your area a bit huh?”, Bernie said, without correcting his greeting.

The other programmer sighed and walked back to his station to pick up the box of crackers he left for himself for later. It was an unwritten rule that Bernard Douglas was the head programmer. He had the biggest console, was involved with the original programs, and even worked on other major projects including the massive cloning lab from PsyClone Industries along with their competitor NeuroRex. He had the clout, and he knew it, and he didn’t care much for people doing things their own way, only his. He could request for someone’s file to be reviewed as a security breach and it would be honored, and even the central computer would process Bernie’s work as priority. While the clout may be used in less than altruistic ways, Mr. Douglas’ work was extremely advanced. While no one could out think the Central Processor, Bernie could design entities that could match it. By working backward or jump-starting certain computing necessities with logic or good intuitive assumptions, often times Bernie could reach an accurate conclusion before the computers did, with some sacrifice to a perfect average. Overall, of course, the computers would out do him consistently, but from time to time, Bernie would get close with his own mechanisms and his own computational elements.

Once Wendell got all of his left overs and stumbled out of the lab office, Bernie spun around on his chair and wheezed. He turned on the computers and started loading up his programs to where he left off two weeks ago. He started working immediately, getting caught up with several programs at once, coming up with new ways to program the locking mechanism on the doors, to a better way to algorithmically determine if an inmate had enough salt in their diet. Bernie sat crunching data and looking at outputs, creating new elements and testing them on his private server then submitting finished results to the central computer to check, recheck, test, and integrate into the PCF master program files, the files that ran Paris. Once every couple of days or every couple of half days, Bernie would get tired. He'd find himself sleeping in his chair, or head back to a small room behind him with a cot and attached full bathroom He'd lounge in there, and sleep, or loudly masturbate, eat, or think through a program's error messages. He'd eventually get up a few hours later and return to his console, eagerly working through bugs, fixes, and codes that the central computer sent back to him, or that he had found on his own. For those two weeks, Bernie and Paris would be working side by side.

Ally walked through the corridor as Dr. Amir and A.I.L., who was rolling along with his own tripod of wheels, stepped up to the entry way of Paris. The mechanics outfitted AIL's briefcase with extendable legs that were motorized. AIL could zip around with the tour without the mechanics for now. The car ride had been uncomfortable as very few words were said, and the memory of the other invitee being cast out of the tour group fresh in their minds, the patrons sat in their seats mostly quietly. Some could not help but murmur now and then especially as the many signs posted, "DO NOT ENTER, GOVERNMENT FACILITY, WITHOUT PROPER REMOTE CLEARANCE YOU WILL BE SHOT ON SIGHT" appeared out their window. The tour group within Ally's car asked about the ethics of such a sign, and if it would be held up in court. Some asked if anyone would ever be stupid enough to actually test that theory. Ally didn't need to think about getting over the gate for right now, she just needed to get inside.

As they emptied out of the cars, and followed the tour guidelines. Dr. Amir explained that the security protocols were recently re-written, and in order to have a tour at all there were major risks involved.

"It is of the utmost importance that you are registered into the central computer on its own terms so doors will open for you, and that you will not be seen as a wild entity. Please put your finger here for your biometric scan, and a tracker device." Dr. Amir motioned to the small security outpost where a machine sat. As the tour group walked up one by one putting their fingers on the biometric scans and stepped away, one of Ally's colleagues asked, "What is the tracker device precisely, Doctor?"

"Oh, they are a series of nano bots that exist within your body. Do not worry, they will be eliminated from the body after a few days along with your bodily waste. They do, however, need to be accompanied by these fashionable necklaces" Dr. Amir continued, as he took out a small ring from the security booth, typed in a few digits and connected it around the neck of someone who had already gone through the biometric stand. The colleague looked at Ally and whispered, “Those look like collars, not necklaces, what are we animals now?”. Ally smiled humoring her, but ultimately trying to remember what else she had heard about nanobot technology.

Ally stood in front of the security machine and placed her finger on the metric scan. Immediately A.I.L. lit up and moved over to her. “Have you ever been in this facility before?”
Ally, who was sufficiently startled whispered, then cleared her throat, speaking clearly, “No- No, I haven’t”. A.I.L. seemed to ignore her response and move toward Dr. Amir, stating, “Continue with the tour, Doctor.”. Ally was one of the last ones to receive her necklace, and caught up with the others as Dr. Amir began explaining the lights that lit up the ground as they walked. Ally tried to keep up and listen but was distracted by the large closing solid steel doors that closed behind them in the sally port. Before she realized it, she was at the mercy of Paris.

Shawn couldn’t help but laugh at Frank attempting over and over to shield his collar from the cameras above him. The localized speaker told him over and over to keep his hands at his sides while walking, but Frank continued to try to scratch his neck, or smooth out his hair as he stepped off the line, only to get shocked and reminded to stay in line. While Shawn couldn’t help but laugh at Frank’s stupidity, he could time how long the computer seemed to take in administering two different consequences at once. One for ignoring the proper posture while walking, and for two, stepping off the line entirely. Shawn could tell the consequences increased as Frank continued to do it over the course of the day, Frank seemed to continue to try only when Shawn began to push him.

"I'm getting close, you see? When you held your hand higher in the air and blocked more of your neck with your arm, the consequence came two seconds later!", Shawn would lie to Frank later during free time.

"Ah! Exactly!" Frank would exclaim, certain he was getting closer to the mystery.

"There's something I'm close to, though, really close to, but I'm not sure if I'm on the right track or not…." Shawn trailed off, hoping Frank would bite.

"What do you mean? You're close to figuring out how it all works?" Frank responded, eagerly.

"Yeah, I mean, I think so… Maybe. I just need to test duration."

"Duration…you mean how easily something breaks?" Frank asked,

"No no, that's durability, I mean how long something lasts…" Shawn stated, still trying not to sound like an authority. It was critical the Frank continued to believe that he was in charge, and that Shawn was working for him in order to solve Frank's goals.

"Oh, right duration. Yes. Well, we're only here for a few more months I think…." Frank trailed off as if giving Shawn actual information.

"Ah, you're right Frank. But what I mean is that I need to see how long the consequences last. Maybe it's a set timer or something."

"Ah! Of course! The laser can only trigger a consequence for so long! Otherwise, another laser would have to set off the thing again! Perfect! So, all we have to do is get someone to withstand the consequence long enough to see how long until the second laser hits the collar setting off another consequence making it feel longer than it is!" Frank stated excitedly, but still in a hushed tone. Spies, remember.

Shawn smiled a little, trying to look serious, but could not help laughing at this idiot inside of his head. Frank started going into details about which other guys he could get to help him cover up his collar the next day when he jumped off the line, and how many other guys would be willing to put up with the consequences enough for the experiment. Shawn nodded and stopped paying attention. All he needed to know was how long the consequence would last and if it wavered at all for an extended time period. How his test subjects kept themselves off the line, or breaking the rules was little consequence to him. One step at a time. But what broke his concentration wasn't the lack of interest, it was Shakeem, walking through the double doors and being led to the free time area. They hadn't talked in a while, but Shawn had seen Shakeem watching him from time to time.

What was it? What made his treatment specialist act so bizarre? What made the central computer believe he was doing better? What changed....? Something to do with that Shawn kid, sure, and something about helping him out, fine. What do I do now? What should I change? If I go forward, I could end up going backward; I could get too attached, too frustrated, end up doing something stupid. If I do nothing, I could stay here forever...

There was a loud “Clank” next to Shakeem as he thought to himself in the cafeteria. Another resident slammed his tray down on the table too hard. It was a veteran resident, one Shakeem knew pretty well. The ‘clank’ must’ve been just barely too loud because a small localized voice stated, “Please be gentle with all materials and equipment”, without a consequence. The boy formed a cross across his chest and bowed, as if praying for forgiveness, and smiled. The other boys at the table laughed. Shakeem gave a smile and shook off his thoughts. Even if he was doing something different that he wasn’t aware of, it was probably in his best interest to just be himself. Two weeks of doing what he was already doing didn’t seem so bad. If he saw Shawn again, he would talk to him, and try to be nice. Maybe that’s all he had to do; just be nice to Shawn.

Later in recreation, Shakeem found Shawn within a black-lined area for a game of basketball. Shawn greeted Shakeem, but kept his focus on the game. Shakeem felt a strange nervousness. He tried to act normal, which often had the opposite effect.

“Uh, yeah.. Hey… Shawn”, he hesitated and stumbled over his words.

“Uh huh?”, Shawn grunted as he caught the ball and passed it to another player.

“So, can I get in? You know next game or what?” Shakeem stated, a little less nervously.

“Well, next we’re playing three on three, but after that I don’t know”, Shawn said, still distracted. He didn’t seem interested at all in Shakeem anymore. Shakeem shrugged and walked away a few steps, watching the game play on the sidelines. He watched Shawn, but more importantly, he watched as the next game started. Shawn was practically militant.

“We’re not letting those fuckers win another one, do you understand?” Shawn said in a low stern voice. The other boys grunted, “Fuck No!”

The game started and his team was aggressive. Not too hard, not too rough, no consequences or warnings were given out, or at least none that Shakeem could hear. Shawn checked the ball hard, hard enough to just almost hit his opponent in the chin. His opponent caught the ball just in time, but looked crossly at Shawn. “You playing or not?” Shawn would ask sarcastically when his opponent would pause for a second- perhaps using his learned anger management coping skills. Shawn would disrupt his thinking by reaching for the ball and provoking him, “If you aren’t going to play, then go sit on the bleachers with the rest of the women, faggot.” The other boy would laugh it off, and continue to dribble, trying to shake off the obvious insult and continue the game.

Shakeem watched, wondering what the point of this was. Shakeem imagined Shawn getting punched in the face, and them both being shocked into submission. What would be the point of that? The other boy was clearly bigger than Shawn, and in the middle of a game who is to say the central computer would miss an elbow to the side, or a jab of the knee? Most of the time, the boys in the facility don’t try to fight each other, unless they’re brand spankin’ new. But by the time they reach recreation hours, they know how things work. Yet, Shakeem thought, if a boy was purposefully trying to start a fight, or wanted to finish some unfinished business from out of the street, it’s possible he would be dumb enough to try it on the recreation floor.

That’s when Shakeem noticed that Shawn wasn’t the only other one provoking other players. “……Faggot!”, another boy said from across the room. Shakeem looked over and saw the other three games going on, four in total including Shawn's. They were being just as aggressive, just as rude and provoking as Shawn was.

"…. your momma!'

"…. suck this dick!"

"…. you and your sister"

"…. because you're a bitch like that"

More and more comments, jabs, excessive clapping when someone shot a ball, excessive celebration when one team scored. Just every little thing to make the opposing team feel worse. Not only that, Shakeem noticed, it wasn't every boy, it was only six or seven at the most who were the worst offenders. Now, over time, some of the boys would bark back, and sheepishly make postures, still aware of the array of cameras watching their every movement. But as they continued to play, show off, and mouth off, no consequences were given out. They were just under the threshold of consequences for a black-lined area. Shakeem had done his fair share of testing limits before. He had his moments of saying words just close enough to curses to get shocked, or pretend to punch people, or throw something just to see what counted as a gesture or not. Typically, he found that it was a fairly arbitrary concept to him personally. He may receive a consequence for calling someone a 'Ditch" in a forceful way, but not a consequence for calling someone a 'bitch' calmly under his breath when he was merely stating the word. Shakeem assumed the cameras and the people behind them didn't care about the words themselves, but just the attitude or the act of aggression itself. He didn't put too much thought in it after that.

Before Shakeem could notice, Shawn made a shot, missed, and when it was his turn to check the ball again, passed it to his teammate. Shawn yelled, "NOW",

Consequences began immediately.

As each of the six or seven aggressive boys attempted to throw their ball at their chosen opponent, swing a fist, tackle, or kick another guy on the court, and as that opponent moved to respond in kind with a defensive block, a punch, or a kick, they all but fell to the ground after barely any contact. The residents began to writhe in pain as they rolled on the floor, some of them trying to cover their necks with their hands, but inevitably clutching their stomachs, legs, and hearts. The screams and wails of pain, along with the obligatory cursing and weeping followed. And as the boys around Shawn and Shakeem fell, the two boys locked eyes for a second, Shakeem a look of terror as the entire room seemed to descend into chaos, and Shawn, a small smirk.

Just as Shakeem processed Shawn's facial expression they both fell to the ground immediately. Shawn felt as though he was punched in his lungs, and there was simply no air to breathe while also being punched in the stomach, and the back of the knees. Shakeem suddenly felt as though his legs disappeared and crumbled beneath him and when he moved his muscle spasms increased and his spine lit up as if on fire. The two immediately forgot their thoughts and feelings for a moment as they gasped, twitched, and struggled for relief. Shakeem stopped moving after a few seconds, recognizing the pattern.

"A 60 second consequence for aggressive intent and behavior. Please be mindful of your interactions with other residents. Thank you!", the speakers bellowed from the recreation hall. The localized speakers on each collar repeated this phrase verbatim. The only variation was in Shakeem and Shawn's collar. Shakeem's stated, "Please remain still while order is re-established". And Shawn's collar said, "Not too bright kid….", in a deep male voice followed by a wheeze.

Bernie was working on the new inputs from the external city files his colleagues at PsyClone asked him to process. Apparently, some from Dr. Zyneburg himself, head of cloning development and engineering. This could mean big things if he could integrate city-wide files with his central processor, he just had to make sure the data array wasn't going to interfere with the behavior of the central processor at Paris. This means examining the stream as they were forged, but he wasn't there when the streams started… Wendell was. He hated that the timing was wrong, but he went back to double check the work regardless, he wouldn't want to let Zyneburg down.

While he worked, there was a sudden explosion of activity on one of his monitors. Consequences were being administered constantly, above the normal boundary. He quickly pulled up the data file and read the information in real time. The collars of many residents were being deactivated in the recreational area due to a fight. These weren't riots, aggression toward the building or equipment, but toward other residents. Bernie found this very odd. Residents typically do not fight each other. He pulled up the camera feeds and saw two residents standing. He set lock down protocol one, which sent everyone into a consequence if they were not automatically earning one for safety and control purposes. He took a closer look, however and recognized one resident as 3022, and the other a resident he never noticed before. He selected that resident with a few clicks, and saw his heart rate, vocal patterns, and frontal lobe capacity recent history was way higher than any of the other boys during this period of recreation, the perfect pattern of a heavy thinker. Whereas the computer typically shows an increase of muscle memory execution in the cerebellum and parietal cortex during recreational activity, this resident was all gray matter, all processing. This kid was planning. Bernie grunted and pulled up the localized message conduit. He leaned over into the microphone after selecting Shawn's collar and sent him a small message.

Aaliyah followed along with the tour, hearing Dr. Amir drone on about the specifics of the outer hull of the administration building. She was wondering what she could do next; Maybe sneak away from the tour group and hide somewhere. No… the cameras in this place would see her and someone would notice if she was gone. Maybe she could smash Dr. Amir over the head and somehow take him hostage. No… there were enough people to overpower her, and there's no reason to think she could even handle Dr. Amir on her own. Aaliyah frowned to herself as Dr. Amir continued, "There are four observation decks, one on each side of the interior of the building, along with special extraction units ready at a

moment's notice in case there is an emergency or a problem the central processor cannot handle…"
"… However, that has never been the case since Paris began.", Dr. Amir paused to look at the confused and questioning faces of the tour. "Well, since our restart just half a decade ago. Since then, we haven't had any major problems that the central processor couldn't reconfigure." He turned back to lead the way with A.I.L slowly rolling beside him. A.I.L's light was blinking in a slow calming pulse of muted blue once more.
The tour reached a break in the hallway. A sign pointed in both directions. To the right: Observation Deck One. To the left: Elevator. Dr. Amir took a sharp left and the tour followed. Suddenly A.I.L stopped moving for a moment, and the light turned a solid deep blue. As the other tour members continued walking A.I.L. stood still letting them pass until Aaliyah took a step closer to him. Suddenly, as she reached the side of the device, the floor lit up with a beautiful blue glow. A line of light lit up and the tour group gasped at the sudden change. Dr Amir looked over to A.I.L. and Aaliyah, who both stopped together behind the tour group.

"A.I.L… What are you doing?", Dr. Amir stated slowly.
"Ms. Aaliyah Shakeem has been requested in a different part of the facility." A.I.L. responded quickly, anticipating the question.
"Me?" Ally hesitated speaking, still thinking about what happened when the other tour member spoke out of turn. She also wondered if the computer knew she was related to an inmate. A.I.L. turned to face Ally and stated in a somewhat quieter voice, "This isn't where you are supposed to be."

Ally thought about her brother, about what he was going through and what she could possibly do to save him. She thought about how she had no plan after getting into the facility, and how she seemed at the mercy of Paris already. The wide spacious white hallways with windows along both sides seemed to be closing in on her slowly forcing her to make a decision that seemed trivial to the other tour members, as they shuffled into the elevator. Dr. Amir looked at A.I.L., then to Ally in the hallway, then to the eager and distinguished guests he had to entertain. He didn't know what protocol AIL was operating under, but he would check after the main tour was over.

After another "Ding" from the elevator as the numbers encrusted on the panel rose from L to 2, A.I.L. asked once more, "Are you ready?", and without hearing an answer, turned, and rolled around the corner. Ally scratched her neck nervously, where the necklace glowing the same blue light as the ground rested. She sighed, realizing she had no real choice and followed A.I.L. around the corner.

Protocol after a massive consequence apportionment is a cool down period where residents are led back to their rooms. Other activities for the day are put on hold, and the system recalibrates for errors. For Shakeem and Shawn, it meant they sat in their rooms for hours doing nothing.

Once the central computer is finished fully calibrating for the incident, reports are filed for those involved and sent to the treatment specialists along with any other relevant entities. The residents are let out and updated on their sentencing if there is a significant change.

After around 3 hours of doing nothing, sleeping, and doing more of nothing, the residents were led out to the free time areas on the clusters. They lazily stepped into the black boxes laid out across the cluster and sat in the couches, watched TV, and stretched out. Shawn, Frank, and a few of the other boys who were part of the fight were standing and sitting talking in soft whispers. Shakeem walked straight over to them and made his way through the crowd. He faced Shawn, who was sitting on the couch in the center of the other boys standing around him.

"What the hell was that Shawn." Shakeem asked as a statement.

"W-what do you mean?" Shawn replied, trying to hold back a smile.

"Look, you might think this is all a game, but the rest of us are trying to get out of this place alright?" Shakeem said. Frank turned to Shakeem, "What do you think we're trying to do?" Frank stated a bit louder than the whispers from before. The other boys nodded, "you think we're just going to sit here until some computer tells us we can or can't go home? You haven't seen Shawn's plan so you don't know, but we're busting out of here", Frank looked back at Shawn for support, only to be met with Shawn's sharp disapproving glare.

"Look, what he means is…." Shawn began, standing up moving over to Shakeem, "we have to understand what the facility is. We don't know what the connection is between the cameras, or the consequences, or these collars, or whatever it all means, but we need to know how it works. We aren't trying to 'break out' or anything," he looked at Frank again, who was nodding, then back to Shakeem, "we're just trying to understand. You can understand that right?" Shawn smiled weakly.

Shakeem wanted to spit in Shawn's face. "No, you fucker, that's not how it works. You don't subject people to torture just because you 'want to understand'. You can't pick fights in here to satisfy some curiosity for yourself. You can't have people hurt just because you want to know something. I don't know many more months you have in here, but you aren't going to get out by breaking the rules. Follow the rules, and you get out. I've seen it hundreds of times. Fuck around and act out, and you're extended. Don't be an asshole and bring everyone else down with you." Shakeem walked off toward the edge of the square and sat on an empty couch away from the others.

Shawn looked at the other guys he was speaking to, and they looked back at him, and then at each other. "He has a point, we did get a lot of guys a consequence, and then lock the whole facility down for the day just because we wanted to test Shawn's plan…" Frank started. Shawn jumped in, "But that's just it… I think I saw a weakness" Shawn stopped, "… or should we stop so people don't get hurt?"

Frank and the other boys stood or sat looking around uneasy, "Well, what is the weakness?"

"I don't want to speak another word of this if we're going to stop testing this system. Either we're all in this for the long run, or we stop entirely. I understand what Shakeem said, but he's wrong. We're doing this *for* the other boys as well as ourselves. Yes, some may get hurt, but after the consequences we feel fine afterward. It's just a few seconds or so of pain, and we've all experienced pain in our lives. It's a matter of pride! We aren't just animals in a cage, unaware of the tools that control us. If we're going to be caged, we better damn well know the limits of the cage, the depth of our stay, and the blind spots of our oppressors!"

The other boys didn't know what Shawn was talking about, but the feelings were conveyed through Shawn's resolve. The boys nodded and Frank agreed, "We do this for everyone. Shawn, what's the plan?"

Shawn tried to hold back a triumphant smile. Manipulating these idiots was easier than he thought. He had persuaded them to be slowly more aggressive over the last few days during recreation just to see where the limits were for consequences. He had convinced a few boys in each cluster to go along with the plan, with Frank's help of course. And he had timed it all perfectly to happen all at once during the basketball game to provoke other boys not in the plan to release their pent-up frustration into a large fight, a real one. Shawn took careful notice of the order in which the boys fell to the ground, and the pattern in how they fell. Shawn noticed how the boys held which body part first or second or third, still trying to figure out how a collar can trigger these feelings all over the body. None of these findings would actually mean anything to the other boys, and none of what he found was enough to change behavior or protect them against consequences. Shawn knew that in order to keep this going, he had to show true results, or at least something they could grasp onto.

"Gentleman, I believe there was a delay between consequences… some got consequences before others and I think the pattern was based on who was closest to the doors…" Shawn started. The other boys nodded, and 'ooed' as this new information was given out. It felt like story-time to Shawn, where the next chapter of the storybook was revealed to expectant toddlers. “I believe, if we stand as far away from the doors as we can, there will be a more significant delay in consequences, and maybe, in the right context, we could find a weak wall, or something to tunnel out of here” Shawn concluded. The boys looked confused. “Tunnel?... With what? …. Did he say tunnel?... What?”.. the boys murmured to themselves, unconvinced. Frank chimed in, “Well, I’m not sure about tunneling, but something! This is good news! We found a weakness!” The other boys nodded and made small celebratory noises. Shawn and Frank looked at each other and nodded. Frank added to the group, “Also, I’m not sure they’re using lasers at all anymore, it could be something else.” The rest of the boys also nodded, some of them reaching that conclusion ages ago. Shawn didn’t tell them about the voice he heard from his collar, and he didn’t really want to think about it either. However, it did mean that someone was watching him personally, and they knew what he was up to. He had to be more careful.

Or maybe more chaotic.

It didn’t make sense to Bernie. The data was way to extensive to be profitable for just Paris. The city was siphoning processing power to undergo their own filing system rather than using the processor for just Paris and operating the facility. Bernie purged old files and created dumps for redundancies, but none of that created the space he needed for the files the city wanted stored and analyzed. Luckily the Central Computer already started using the reserve memory and processing power, and was in no risk of failing any processes or programs. Bernie tried a few tricks he picked up in combining files to save storage space and just creating a more advanced search and labeling system. Instead of having two files, for let's say resident 1 and resident 2, he would combine ten residents into one longer file and create more specific search terms. He made it easier to find resident 1 and 2 within the single file. The minor difference in processing power to open one file and search versus opening each individual file to search was minor, yet across the trillions of files and programs and applications, the difference was ample. Bernie worked tirelessly since the city's files were combined, and in his spare time he wrote the report to the city governance and the Department of Justice to what the issues were in combining these files. He was so busy readjusting the program while keeping it running during major consequence events and the normal running of the facility, that he almost forgot about watching the tour group's progression through the facility. He kept one eye on Dr. Amir as he walked through the second floor, showing the tour group how the collars worked and how the residents walked through the lines. There was a mini-example for those who wanted to experience a weak consequence, just to prove that it was not fatal or anything an average teenager could not handle, and to show that after the consequence was completed, there were no side effects. The tour group seemed to be pleased and the reporters jotted down notes eagerly. Bernie shook his head, thinking about how the glory of the facility wasn't in consequences or a schedule. It was in the predictive and calculatory power of the computer running it all. His system *knew* a person. Truly understood a person inside and out. From heartbeat to hunger, this computer could calculate what a person would be craving and give it to them before they realized it. Bernie was proud of his machine, and happy the government saw its potential. Something, however, was wrong. When he looked at the files Zyneburg had given him, there was a duplication in one of the resident's files that was not listed as an abnormality. This one file had two different names, and when Bernie tried to delete one, it repopulated from the original source. He reached out to Zyneburg himself for clarification, but the line was always busy or down. Bernie tried to isolate the file but could not do anything to it that created a lasting change. Bernie figured it was a core file, just in the wrong location, and decided to leave it alone for now. The duplication was for a resident J. Shakeem and A. Shakeem, but in the registry, there was no A. Shakeem listed, and the file only appeared after the merge. Bernie marked the glitch, and flagged it for the Central Processor to look at for redundancies and query but at a low importance level. There were other things a bit more pressing than tracking down an individual resident file. "Probably just an old file the computer is referencing for a moment. Sometimes the computer does a history check. When it's done it'll put the file back where it belongs." Bernie told himself as he wheezed, and took a bathroom break.

Ally followed A.I.L. quietly, hearing the whirr of the rotors and motors in the wheels of the device ahead of her. "Where are we going…?" Ally finally asked, but A.I.L. said nothing as he wheeled past the observation deck and past another sign labeled “Intake Pavillion.” Ally felt a chill down her spine. A.I.L. finally spoke. “This is where you belong.” Ally stopped walking, “What do you mean? Why are we going to the Intake?”

“We’ve made a terrible mistake. We must correct this at once!” The blue light shimmered around A.I.L. as the Pavilion doors opened and the liaison lady cheerfully welcomed them.

“Hello! So nice to finally meet you! Before we begin, I will need you to drink this!” The liaison sang as she brought Ally a blue vial of thick liquid. Ally looked around the room a bit confused again, seeing operating tables around her in this white room. “Wh-what is it for?” Ally hesitated trying not to sound defiant, but also not willing to poison herself either.

“It’—” The liaison started,

“It’s a substance that allows maximum health while traversing this facility any deeper. To reach where you need to go, it is necessary to avoid radiation of the computers and other bioelectrical feedback. No human being passes this point without this treatment.” A.I.L. stated simply.

Ally looked at the vial and took it from the liaison, and drank it. Deeper into the facility is exactly where Ally wanted to go. The taste was awful and thick, the whiff of metal and rust filled her nostrils, but she produced enough saliva to swallow all of it. A.I.L. turned to the liaison and said, “Proceed.”

Shakeem was dreaming. He was floating again, unable to tell which way was up or down. He was horizontal. He could not tell where he was, or which direction to move in, but there was pressure. It built up slowly at first, a small pulse of a push in all directions. He moved his arms, his legs, and felt he was in a liquid. He immediately tried to breathe; he couldn't. He began to panic. He flailed his arms and legs, and more pressure. He heard crying, far away, distant crying, muted, muffled, crying. The pressure increased. The liquid started to rush by him as the pressure increased, he couldn't breathe, but he could see the sides of the container closing in on him as he was thrusted in one direction. The crying became louder and louder as he was pushed through. He could breathe, and realized he was the one crying all along. He couldn't see. Just darkness. But warmth. He was warm, and breathing, and he stopped crying.

The warmth moved away, and he found himself back in the open, horizontal, floating. He slowly opened his eyes to see the red eye of his room at Paris, staring at him.

Shakeem woke up. "Good morning residents…." The daily greeting started. Shakeem tried to shake off the dream but it was a recurring one. The openness of the air, the feeling of liquid around him, the pressure and warmth; it all felt familiar and distant. He usually was able to shake off these feelings by breakfast. While he sat at his table, he noticed Shawn and the other boys talking again at their table. This time more boys from other pods were joining in.

Bernie watched the monitor closely, seeing the boys cluster together in the cafeteria. He swung his chair over to look at the readout from the computer and the current assessment of the situation. The readout seemed negative overall but the stipulation of the black outline was causing the processor to second-guess itself. Bernie decided to lower the consequence sensitivity of the black outlined areas slightly, to give the computer more room to judge and consequent. Given the readouts for this particular resident, 6301 SHAWN AIKMAN, there seemed to be a special case presented. He gave the computer permissions to consequent and command 6301 specifically. Bernie checked 6301's disposition statement and noticed that his profile included high intelligence and fondness of manipulation. Then decided to program this feature into future cases as well. Bernie wanted the troublemaker silenced.

Suddenly, Shakeem saw Frank and the other boys jump up and run toward the giant window in the cafeteria, some standing in front of each other, their backs against the window. Shawn stayed seated, watching the boys and nodding. Shakeem shook his head and stood up to confront Shawn.

"Not again! Shawn! Quit it! Now!"

"Just stay out of this Shakeem, you're messing with the experiment!" Shawn growled back,

“Residents it is time now to line up for the next activity. Please clean up your area and line up.” The overhead speakers chimed as the purple light lit up along the floor.
“Here it comes!” Frank said to everyone standing on the wall,
“Remember! Resist all you can!”
Shakeem took a step toward the line instinctively, but hesitated, “Shawn, you don’t know what you’re doing, you have to cut this shit out. This shit isn’t a game!”
Shawn stood up to face Shakeem, but doubled over in pain. He clutched his stomach and fell to the ground. Frank and the other boys watched, confused, as they were expecting pain but received none.
Shakeem looked around and then back at Shawn, “Shawn, they’re watching us, you have to give it up, tell everyone to get back in line.”
Shawn mumbled through gasps of pain, “None… of.. this.. is real… remember? It’s.. All.. Fake…”
Shakeem paused for a moment, remembering the words he spoke to Shawn earlier, and took a step back as the overhead speakers gave out another warning of impending consequences.
“….. 30 seconds until consequences”
Shawn writhed on the floor until his thoughts became distorted. Suddenly he felt relief. He was able to stand up.
Frank looked at Shawn nervously, unsure of whether the protest should be called off. Shawn shook his head defiantly, a stern look that said “You better not quit”. Frank nodded, as he counted down. Shakeem joined the line with the others who were confused about what was going on. He stood on the purple line and turned his head to face forward, away from the cries

of pain that began behind him. Shawn's throat seized next, Frank and his friend's legs buckled as they fell to the floor. They clutched their throats and tried to endure. After a mere fifty seconds of being unable to breathe, and being unable to move the consequences vanished. Many of the boys crawled, rolled, and ran to the line. Frank, Shawn, and three others remained. The boys in line knew to be quiet. To speak during transition would be given a consequence. They simply had to listen. The consequences started up again. Frank and the boys ended up crawling to the line, followed by a defeated Shawn.

The cafeteria rebellion was over.

Bernie looked at the data and decided to decrease the pain limitation across the board. He checked and double checked to make sure any current resident had no outstanding health issues, and maintained the pain thresholds for those individuals who were special cases. He would keep an eye of those cases to see if there was a spike in mortality risk by percentage, but as long as it stayed under 25% for cases 5501, 3324, 3022, and 1223, he would be able to let the computer increase pain allotments indefinitely until indications of compliance.

The job was the make the computer as self-sufficient as possible. It wasn't enough to combat the issue at hand. Bernie's job was to make the computer able to adjust appropriately. Every time Bernie adjusted the computer based on a situation, the computer learned what to do if the situation would occur again. When Bernie made adjustments, the computer would look at all relevant data and copy the situation in order to know a protocol for next time. Bernie was very careful to place into practice only the protocols that would be permissible at any future moment. Bernie's job was to create a system that didn't need him anymore; 100% fully automated facility.

While the boys slept, Bernie often watched the cameras at night as well. He would watch as the computer analyzed the building for weakness, structural damage, and pathogens. Cleaning bots would roam the hallways to clean scuff marks, left over contaminants in the cafeteria, and straighten up areas in the education pavilion. Specialized robots would be in the gym to inflate basketballs and arrange activities for the next day. Bernie oversaw these activities looking for ways to better equip the computer with the tools it needed to function indefinitely. The "Night Crew" as Bernie put it, seemed to be very efficient at what they did, and little needed to be adjusted from night to night. Bernie looked at the clocking system from his own frame of reference to that of the Facility.

Ally woke up in a small room, and immediately noticed a collar around her neck. She looked around frantically for someone, anyone. She tried to calm herself down. Deep breaths.

Part 3

Snitches III

"No, it isn't torture at all. Research shows that you only need 6-8 hours of sleep a night. So, we just went off of that. Why not make a day 16 hours rather than 24? You think it really matters to the inmates? If the facility runs twice as fast, the residents get their time done faster, see? It's not a bad idea when you think of it. The residents aren't the wiser- No clocks or real windows see? Time is just a shitty construct, isn't it? Isn't that what the undereducated say? So, just repeat that to yourself and go back to your day. There's no way you can get me to say that adjusting time references is bad.

"So we use the same words, big deal! A day is just what we call it. A Paris minute is just half as long as an Earth minute. Probably a fraction of the Mars minute, and way longer than a Mercury minute. So who fucking cares? It's all relative. The point remains the same. Keeping the residents on our time keeps them in control. They sleep when we tell them to sleep, not when they feel like it. They remain rested, or sleep deprived when we want them to be. It's all part of the psychological process of rehabilitation. Think about it- If you were trying to lose weight, wouldn't it make sense to have longer recreation times, and shorter meal times? But if 30 minutes of one is the same as 30 minutes of the other, then you might not see enough progress. If you felt you were working out for 30 minutes, but it was really an hour, and you felt you had a long lunch break of 30 minutes, but it was really 15, you might end up getting results twice as fast, see?

"It's the same thing with these punk kids. They think they're getting a full night's sleep and short education periods. They think they're having recreation and free time, but it's all manipulated by the day and their profiles. The computer does it all. The best part is, once you lose your frame of reference, which most residents do after a week of being in the facility, it's almost impossible to spontaneously get it back. We all "sort of know" how long five minutes is. But without any feedback for a week, you lose that ability easily! It's not so bad when you think of it. Imagine how happy a company would be to give their employees a two-hour lunch break? As long as they stay within the building, the profits would stay the same, if you know what I mean."

Dr. Amir walked quickly from the entrance of the building, just leaving the tour group by the security sentry. The tour members placed their hands in the machine and their modified necklaces were unlatched and returned to the security bin. Dr. Amir walked to his office and did a search for A.I.L. and Aaliyah. A.I.L. was charging in a port by the Intake Pavilion, Aaliyah's security necklace had been deactivated. She was gone. He walked to the Intake Pavilion and found A.I.L., his light grey and lifeless. He pushed the power button on the side of the case and A.I.L. sprung to life his light looking bluer.

"Hello Doctor." the liaison said.

"A.I.L., Where is that one tour member, did she go by security? The tour group is leaving now." Dr. Amir said.

"She will not be leaving Doctor." A.I.L. said.
"What? She has to leave; the cars are leaving now." Dr. Amir stated, not understanding.
"The protocol is clear, Doctor. She cannot leave the facility until the main computer has thoroughly processed her psychological profile and she has been rehabilitated."
"She isn't a resident; she is a tour group member. Where is she now?"
"Resident A. Shakeem 4495 is in lockdown. She may not have visitors." A.I.L. said. There was a silence for a moment as the words hung in the air. Dr. Amir repeated these words in his head, as his brain finally connected meaning to each one.
"Wh.. What did you do?" Dr. Amir whispered as he turned to run down the hall back toward the elevator.
"Please no running Dr. Amir" the overhead speaker stated as Dr. Amir continued toward the programmer offices and the control room.

Dr. Amir tried to use his pass but he forgot he needed both programmer and external visitor authorization. He had to wait for Bernie to open his side of the door as well.
Bernie looked up from watching the monitors of his cleaning robots and noticed commotion at his door. He saw the readout as Dr. Amir, and scoffed. What did the fancy doctor want to talk to him about now, his stupid tour group or something? Bernie opened the door and Dr. Amir rushed in.
"Alright, alright, calm down. What is it Doc?" Bernie said sarcastically letting out a sharp wheeze.

“I need you to run a scan on new intakes today.” Dr. Amir stated, breathing in and out heavily.
“Intakes? Today? No way sir. We only get intakes every few weeks, and I have no—”
“I need you to run a scan, please.” Dr. Amir stated again, calmly.
“Doc, I’m telling you…”
“I need you to run the scan.”
Bernie shrugged and slid his chair over to the console to run a scan. He clacked on his keyboard harder than usual, showing true disdain for the Doctor’s request. He looked at the data on the monitor light up as it showed details of the last intakes, but something was wrong.
“W..wait a second” Bernie said, looking at the monitor closely. “This-This isn’t right. How do we have one more intake today? Just now? Just a few minutes ago…” Bernie turned toward Dr. Amir. “What. Did. You. Do.”
Dr. Amir shook his head, “I don’t know what happened. Somehow the artificial intelligence liaison put her through the intake process. It has her confused as a resident.”
“That’s not fucking possible. The DNA codes of each resident are stored when we get them here. There’s no fucking way an outsider’s DNA could be confused with an already established resident.” Bernie snapped.
“Then, your Liaison is busted, Bernie. You must have made a mistake” Dr. Amir said, calculating what to do next.
“Me? You’re blaming me? You think I created a faulty machine? You fucking prick. I created the liaison to directly link with the Central Computer, if the Liaison is wrong the Central computer is wrong, and the Central Computer Is Not Wrong”, Bernie yelled back at Dr. Amir. Dr.

Amir wasn't listening anymore. He moved to the monitors and switched through a few views. "What we need to do now is find her and get her out of here". Bernie looked at the monitors too, but then moved to look at the data. He pulled up the file the computer had populated for A. Shakeem 4495, the newest resident. The crimes listed were set for years before this date. Bernie crossed the references and did a search for all remaining residents and found a match. J. Shakeem 3022. Dr. Amir and Bernie looked at each other.

"Siblings…" Bernie said.

"Twins…" Dr. Amir said.

"Twins?" Bernie said, but they're different sexes, they must be fraternal.

Dr. Amir looked at the data in the file and noticed J. Shakeem's age. "This can't be right. How are they twins if they are years apart in age?

Bernie looked over the data as well. "This is impossible. We really fucked up. We really really fucked up. The Department of Justice is going to shut us down. All my work will be ruined. This is just as bad as when that girl died, or when that other kid killed himself. We'll be tied up in red tape for years."

"Calm down…." Dr. Amir was thinking, "We can claim it was part of a special tour or something. Get her to sign a waiver, even cash if she wants it. This needs to go away quietly."

They were both silent for a while.

The monitors flickered.

Ally followed the red line on the ground toward the cluster and was led to pod A. The line took her to her room where she stepped over the black line. The door closed behind her. She looked around noticing the bare white walls, the cot and the desk along with chair. She also noticed the light and speaker next to her bed. She wasn't sure about anything at the moment, but she was sure she did not want to feel a consequence again. The memory of how deep and sharp the pain in her stomach was for screaming for help in lockdown, or when she tried to make a run for it after the intake prompts. She quickly learned how the inmates were kept in line. She sat on the cot and looked down at her thighs. She thought about her brother being stuck in a place like this. Marching through lines, not being able to speak. Having to change himself so much, when all she ever wanted for him was to be happy and to be himself. She began to cry. Through tears she remembered the day she knew she was getting a little brother. The day she felt so lucky to have someone to look out for. She thought about how she would sacrifice for him, and vouch for him when he did something wrong. She felt more connected with her brother than anyone, really. When her parents died, she was able to use their insurance policy and part time jobs to keep them both happy and comfortable. When her brother started to act out, she understood because she, too, wanted to act out as well. Her responsibility to her brother kept her in line and stable, but now it was just a bunch of consequences and bright lights on the floor. She wept for her brother who took the passing of his parents so hard that he fell into bad habits, hung out with wrong people, and ended up in prison. She wept for the feeling of loss and loneliness she felt as she researched the problems Paris had previously undergone, and the history of death and catastrophic mishaps that occurred within the premises and beyond. She thought about the months she spent to get a chance to be in this very spot, closer to her brother than ever, but also stuck. She slammed her fist on the cot, thinking about how stupid it was to drink that fluid, how dumb it was to leave the tour group. She wanted to write an article about the torture of Paris, the inhumane conditions, the real insider look at what really goes on at Paris from the point of view of an inmate, and maybe get some justice for her brother and every other resident who had been through these doors. Instead, she became a resident herself. This wasn't legal, she thought to herself. But she wasn't in a court room. She was in a cell. Alone.

Dr. Amir and Bernie watched the camera as Ally sat in her room. Bernie suddenly went through the central computer processor and started queries. Dr. Amir called the other programmers to see what changes they had made in the system over the past two weeks. Bernie pulled 3022's file and looked at the relevant changes over the past few weeks and noticed something strange. Under treatment goals it was listed, "demonstrate how to be a good brother". He passed this to Dr. Amir, who read it and continued talking on the phone. Bernie looked at the records 4495 and 3022 had in common and noticed that their DNA only showed up together in one other file, an external file.

".... Zyneburg..." Bernie said, as his hands left the keyboard, the monitor flickering with information in front of him. Dr. Amir put down the phone and hunched over the console. “This is not good, none of them have any information. We should at least disable her chip so she can’t have consequences and just keep her there until we can get an extraction team to get her out of there.”

“No... the Computer wouldn’t allow it”. Bernie stated, defeatedly through a long wheeze, “The central computer will not allow a resident to escape the facility, we cemented that feature in the base code. Until the computer is satisfied that the resident has completed all programming, the resident will remain. In fact, in order to ensure this, we allowed the computer 99% fatality permissions in the event there was a massive break out, or a power failure.” Bernie explained.

“What were we thinking back then…” Dr. Amir sighed, “We were so sure of ourselves.”

“We were competing against other facilities where people were hacking into systems and breaking out. That was our concern back then, not someone getting sealed in. It’s a fucking prison, man, locking people in is the whole fucking point. It just, locked in someone who shouldn’t be here, that’s all. Look, maybe I can reduce consequences to zero, and then mark the case important to the Central Processor, and have it erased both cases, 3022, and 4495, it looks like 3022 only had about a week left anyway. Maybe we could fix them both.” Bernie spun back around to the computer. “But by the way, I think I know what happened… read this.” Bernie handed Dr. Amir a piece of paper he printed off the monitor.

Dr. Amir rubbed his eyes and looked at the paper.

DATE: <Redacted>

TIME: <Redacted>

CASE: 45692-G9

PSYClone Industries Lab 1341 Transcribed Meeting Note

Progress: DNA Sequence of A. Shakeem, Age 4 Transcribed and Duplicated into new host in entirety. DNA Sequence uploaded into chosen identity Jason Shakeem, age 0 with following changes: sex (Y Chromosome synthesis), height potential factor (15% increase), muscle potential (factor x2).

New Host (J. Shakeem) will be synthesized in 4 weeks to allow grief.

Reason listed: Replacement Child for parents Ajanae Shah, and Kyle Kem. Previous child lost due to emotional dysregulation. Parents request replacement entity for sentiment.

Reason approved: Personal favor

DATE: <Redacted>

TIME: <Redacted>

CASE: 45692-G9

PSYClone Industries Lab 1241 Transcribed Meeting Note

Follow up assessment: DNA sequence duplicated successfully, new host growth to potential and ready to be extracted from final enclosure. J. Shakeem will be given citizenship and documented into the city files next week.

DNA sequence 660432261G22 Host

DNA sequence 660432261G22 Clone (relevant data 100% duplicated)

Dr. Amir put down the paper and mumbled. “They’re… clones”.
Bernie didn’t look up, but nodded, still searching through the database and opening queries in the central computer’s never-ending data stream. “Seems like mom and dad kicked the bucket about a decade later, leaving the host, I mean, our newest inmate, to take care of one of our oldest inmates. They must’ve been living together until little cloned brother got locked up. When sister showed up with her identical DNA, the computer registered it as an inmate in the wrong location. Seems like the computer automatically went to correct the issue. This is fucked up.”
Dr. Amir shook his head. “This needs to go away. This needs to go away quickly. I can’t have this station jeopardized, especially if PsyClone is involved. We need to make this go away.” Dr. Amir stated in a calm but stern voice.
Bernie looked up at him, “What the hell are you talking about? We’ve had mishaps before, even dead kids on our hands since a few years ago. What’s another mistake like this really going to do? Don’t we just shuffle some papers around, make a statement and forget about it?”
“You really don’t get it do you,” Dr. Amir began, “Who do you think cleaned up those messes, huh? You think nothing goes on behind the scenes? Why do you think we’re forced to take on the city’s documents

and process half of PsyClone Industry's work? If we show another weakness, the entire premise of automated rehabilitation comes into question. There have been many, many, more incidents outside of what you see on the news. Data by nature is fabricated, and the success of the program is valid, from certain points of view, of course. You don't need to understand everything, I just need these files to disappear." Dr. Amir picked up the paper again and ripped it apart. "I need this done now."

Bernie sat for a moment and thought. He could easily make backups of these files and store it in a hidden folder. The data base is so large that if he changed a few identifiers, no one would ever know it was there but him. Then he considered the opposite, what if he did erase their files. He could retroactively delete their files from PsyClone and the City's DOJ files as well. No one would know they were sentenced here, and no one would know they were here still. They would merely disappear. They had no parents looking for them, and they have no other relatives on file. Who would miss them? Here they get free food, a place to live, exercise... He could assign them to no treatment therapy, so there wouldn't be human contact anymore whatsoever from outside the facility, and if he made up a case file for the central computer, they could be sentenced to indefinite stay.

Dr. Amir interrupted Bernie's thought process, "And when the files are destroyed, give them both extra commissary points. A rat doesn't rattle the cage if it's comfortable." Dr. Amir gritted his teeth and with one motion pushed the bits and pieces of paper into the garbage can. "After this is done, I want to renegotiate your pay and benefits. It's time you got a raise, Bernie." Dr. Amir turned, but his hands in his lab coat pockets, and stepped out of the control room.

Bernie felt torn. Yeah, he was sort of an asshole, but he never made a person disappear before. Handing out consequences to criminals, creating safer and more secure or elaborate security systems sure, but never before did he actually create lasting harm to an individual. It was at this point, when the door closed that Bernie knew what he had to do. He gave the protocol to the computer system to erase files of A. Shakeem and J. Shakeem. He wrote a script for the computer to access files in the city Department of Corrections and Department of Justice files to corrupt and delete any files relating to these individuals. He copied the files into a separate folder and hid it in the Paris computer system and his own mobile device. "for insurance…" he said quietly. He then uploaded these commands to the Paris Central Computer and watched the data work. A and J Shakeem now only existed at Paris under a category of crime "Other" sentenced to infinite years.

He looked at the clock, then at the facility's internal clocking system. It would be 'daylight' soon, and two residents, without even knowing it, will have lost their identity forever. Bernie felt sick.

Everyone was confused on A-Pod. There were many more consequences for talking and holding up the line than ever before. With murmurs and whispers, and boys strained to see what they could not believe. There was a girl here. A woman, really. As they lined up for hygiene, their respective lines were normal, as usual, but Ally decided to keep her clothes on while she showered for obvious reasons. She found the polo shirts a bit too tight, but the pants fit fine. She followed the rules simply enough, always looking around for a particular inmate. She concluded that he was not on A-pod rather quickly, and wondered when she would get to see the other pods. While her primary focus was to see her brother, she was also looking for a way out as well.

As if the shower was awkward enough, she seemed to be at least two to three years older than the boys on her pod, and older still to the rest of the cluster. As she followed in line toward the cafeteria with her own pod and Pod-D, she quickly looked around to see if she could recognize anyone. She couldn't. The line was quiet that morning. Usually at least one or two consequences were administered, even if for a brief moment, but none. Once she stepped over the black line and found a spot by herself, she immediately felt surrounded. Almost every other boy surrounded her with a series of questions, pick-up lines, and dirty jokes (which were immediately, in most cases, given a consequence).

"Hey I can protect you in here,"

"What did you do, with your fine ass?"

"How'd you get locked in here with us?"

"She's got a nice ass, but I'm more about the lips"

"You wouldn't even know what to do with her, move out the way"

"Yo, how *old* are you anyway?!"

"You need a boyfriend?"

"Girl jail is full already huh?"

"Maybe she's a dude that looks like a girl"

"Yeah, she didn't show us the lady bits in the shower either!"
"I'd love to see her squirm from a consequence! Haha!"
"What I wouldn't do with 5 minutes alone with her"
"Guys, just leave her alone",

Ally didn't say a word. If she responded to one, genuine, statement she'd have to respond to all of the statements. She didn't want to make friends, or enemies. She wanted to find her brother and get the hell out of there. She was a reporter for the city newspaper, she was well known throughout the community, and she had at least one friend in politics. Even if she'd have to visit him every night from now on, he could do her another favor and it would be worth it. She just needed to get a message out to him, and then maybe she could end all of this.

Suddenly, a boy behind her fell to the ground with a loud, "AH FUCK!" Ally turned around to see him writhing on the floor. The boy next to him smiled and whispered to her, "He was going to grab your ass. Don't worry, the lasers got him." Ally nodded, and turned back around, then looked up at the cameras along the ceiling. She was glad the system worked, at least for now, she wouldn't have to worry about being raped or molested by horny teenagers. She wouldn't have to be beaten up by angry boys with mommy issues, or guys who just hate women for reasons they don't even understand. Unlike the real world, she didn't have to be molested by powerful people with alternative motives either- no abusive guards, no sexually deprived wardens looking for 'service'. Just cameras, consequences, and time. Lots of time… to think.

No matter how she sliced it, however, she realized she needed help from the inside. Hopefully she could find her brother and they could work out a system together. She had spent her career looking at and studying the facility from the outside. She had learned every spec and every detail about the mechanisms that run the place, or from what little they release to the public. She committed these details to memory in order to better ask questions and know when a politician or a guard was giving her bullshit in an interview. She also studied some of the work of the founders and knew what their overall motivations were. But there was one result she did not quite understand.

Why was she here?

Why did the artificial intelligence liaison put her into the system to begin with? The computer must've found out why she was there, and must've create his own narrative of justice. This would make a great article, she thought. If she could get it to her editors, she could make the headline, "Robotic Justice for Some, Soon for All", she smiled as she finished her toast. Some boys were watching her eat. She ignored them. If she could write an article about how a robotic super computer read her thoughts or created some abstract profile of her, decided that she was intending to break the law, and break someone out of jail, and then decided, without human intervention or approval, to imprison them, there would be an uproar. The public would never allow the idea of super computers making decisions for them and imprisoning people without due process. Human beings will put up with a lot of shit, especially if it makes them comfortable, Ally thought, but infringing on some arbitrary sense of freedom? They'd never allow that.

The speakers began their rant, and Ally lined up with the others. Again, the line was silent as she transitioned toward recreation. After education, they would be returned to the cluster for free time. Ally, of course, didn't participate in recreation. The boys of course showed off, taking risks in the game they wouldn't normally and yelling, "this one is for you girl!" before shooting a shot and bragging about making it to the other guys. Ally wasn't paying attention to the game; she was remembering the processes to how the computer linked with both the neurological processes and the cameras to verify behavior and intention. She wouldn't get a shock if she could 'trip' onto another person by accident, regardless if the person in front of her was hurt or not. She didn't quite understand this while reading about it, but seeing how the lines worked, and seeing how the cameras were positioned, it made complete sense. She just needed to see it in front of her. She needed to live it.

Shakeem heard the rumors. Some chick was admitted into the facility. He didn't really see what the big deal was. Maybe they were integrating girls into the program. He had a fleeting thought about getting to know some of the new female residents, perhaps. Maybe during lunch he'd have a chance to flirt a little. They'd have their own living pod, he was sure. Possibly they'd hang out during recreation and free times. Heck, maybe after their sentence they could meet up in the real world and hang out like normal people. He smiled.

Shawn's voice shook Shakeem out of his trance as he spoke about the introduction of their new peer. "What if she's a spy trying to hear about our plans and report back?" The other boys nodded in thought.

Frank replied, "Yeah, maybe they're trying to get into our secrets and our plans!" Shakeem shook his head. Idiots. Why would they send a girl into do that when a boy would be less conspicuous? It's more likely that Shawn or someone was a spy than anything else, he immediately showed up and started planning shit. Ever since Shawn showed up, he had been causing more consequences and more problems for everyone.

"Alright, I heard she's on Pod-A, all of us guys on Pod-C are going to ignore her, right?" Shawn said.

"Yeah! None of us will talk to her!" Frank said, as the other boys nodded and murmured in agreement.

"I'll check her out to see if she's alright, then I'll let you all know," Shawn said confidently, as if making a deep sacrifice. The other boys nodded and cheered.

How dumb could they be, Shakeem thought. Clearly Shawn just wanted to chat up the girl alone. Poor girl was probably alone and scared and having Shawn talk to her while everyone else ignored her would make Shawn a savior figure. Shakeem smiled at how absurd the whole idea was. Still, he wondered why he cared at all. Shakeem remembered when they first met, how he had tried to help Shawn out a little, explain to him the ropes. Shakeem felt a protective nature about him, maybe because Shawn was so petite and frail, maybe because Shakeem felt so lonely. Maybe because he was just bored. Shakeem shook his head as he thought; maybe he just wanted to feel like a brother again.

Recreation time was over, and they were to return back to the cluster for free time. Sometimes they would mix with D pod, and sometimes they would mix with A-pod, they wouldn't know until they arrived. As they lined up, Shakeem decided not to care anymore. Whoever this new resident was, it was just another resident. She did something wrong, landed herself here, and probably would be out in a few weeks anyway. He didn't think there was much to think about anymore, so he ignored it and went onto thinking about other things.

When he entered the cluster door the yellow line led him to the free space area. He stepped over the black line and found one of his favorite chairs. As the other boys on C-pod settled, the cluster doors opened up once more. "It's A-pod…!" one of the boys whispered, excitedly, and the other boys looked up. Shakeem made it a point to ignore them.

"She's pretty cute"

"Pfft, she's alright."

"Maybe she'll sit on my lap"

"Yeah right, she's like 25"

"Nah, she just looks fully grown"

"Is she a spy? Really?"

"I dunno, let Shawn figure that out"

"Maybe she's married or something"

Shakeem smirked, these idiots are going to get all hyped up and then end up squirming on the ground for being aggressive or getting to close to her or something.

Shakeem looked up, meaning to look at the boys talking, but for a split second something caught his eye. His head moved to the left, as a double take, and he saw her. She was looking at him, staring. He couldn't look away. The other boys looked to see what she was looking at, and saw Shakeem staring back. They immediately started to joke around, but Shakeem couldn't hear them. He couldn't hear anything. Ally followed the green line leading her to the black outlined box for free time, and stepped over the line. The other boys, true to their word tried to move out of her way for Shawn, but the A-pod boys still wanted her attention. Ally ignored them as she walked over to Shakeem. Shakeem stayed seated, not able to process anything.

They stared at each other's identical brown eyes three feet away from each other. Shakeem stood up. The other boys stood quietly and watched, wondering what was about to happen. Shakeem swallowed. Ally's eyes began to tear up. Shakeem looked at the Paris emblem on her polo shirt and felt angry, embarrassed, and confused all at once. Heat on the back of his neck turned to itchy spikes as the feeling crawled down his back making him sweat. Ally's stomach fluttered as she felt sweat on her forehead. She didn't want to move, but she wanted to hold her brother again. She saw him and that horrible collar around his neck and just wanted to rip it off. For a moment she wanted to grab him and run, to sprint through the concrete and steel walls, to crash through the gates, to dodge the bullets from the guard's guns, to dash between the mine field and the auto-turrets and disappear from society forever. For a brief moment she felt like breaking the laws of physics and stepping away from reality with the only person she had in the world.

Shakeem felt heavier. He had to get her out of here. It was all his fault she was here. He had to get her out.

"Why…"

"To find you…"

"But how…"

"I'm not sure.."

"What are you…"

"It's not important…"

"This is fucked up."

"Watch your language."

"You shouldn't be here."

"I know. But I had to be."

"This isn't right."

"This wasn't the plan."

"You don't understand… There's nothing here."

"What do you mean?"

"There's no way out."

"That doesn't matter right now."

"You don't get it."

"I know how this place works."

"I'm not sure you do."

"I'm working on it. Trust me."

"I… I do trust you."

"Good. So, let me think."

"This is really fucked up."

"Yeah….", she laughed. He laughed. She sat down in an empty seat next to him, and he sat back down. They sat in front of the TV playing some black and white old TV show and talked to each other.

"This is kind of weird," one of the other boys said.

"Yeah, I thought she was staring at me this whole time." Another boy said, "No, I mean… I've never seen Shakeem laugh or smile like that before." "Oh, yeah." The other boy said.

Bernie stepped into the office without knocking. Dr. Amir was on the phone.

"Yes, I know that. Yes. The problem is handled. No, you won't be involved. Yes, I understand that. No Sir. Yes, I understand that Sir. No, I won't—Of course sir…."

Bernie looked around the office noticing small trinkets, images of the brain with various structures highlighted. Processes of neurodegeneration and regulation were highlighted on a few. Bernie didn't study the subject extensively, but he knew enough to do his job. He could never program a human, but he could program a computer to program one. After all, he wasn't a people-person. He looked at the antique replicas of skulls under glass, and the antique book collections. He looked at the digital book collections and hologram book cover awards Dr. Amir had personally written. Bernie quietly wheezed through his nose as he thought about what he had to say, and what sort of response Dr. Amir would have.

Dr. Amir sat behind his desk and concluded the call, "You're correct, Sir. Thank you sir." Dr. Amir sighed, and put the phone down. He looked at Bernie and gave a weak smile. "I think we're alright for now. Did you give the two their commissary items?" Bernie nodded and sat down in front of the desk facing Dr. Amir. "Good. Well, given all your work and all your dedication to the project, in addition to this little mishap that you've handled so well, I want to double your salary and a promotion. We do severely appreciate your work, Mr. Bernard." Bernie sat in thought. He knew it would be some grandiose statement like that, but overall, there was little meaning behind it. He already had more money than he knew what to do with. And working on the central computer at Paris was all he ever wanted to do. It was more than enough work to keep him occupied, and it was more than entertaining to find bugs, correct them, and create a more and more progressive machine. He was even working on a few more projects at home. If anything, a promotion just meant managing more people, which he would hate more than he hated Wendell. He shrugged at this offer. It was an insult to who Bernie was a person. Dr. Amir raised his eyebrows slightly, "You don't seem impressed. What would you want?" Bernie wheezed quietly as he thought, and parsed his lips apart. "I think I want to be in charge of the control department…" Bernie began. Dr. Amir interrupted, "Bernie, I don't thin—"

"—… and I don't want any oversight whatsoever. None. I want it to be a black box operation, and I want to design my own goals along with my own protocols. I don't want input from the Psychiatric Association, I don't want oversight from you, or any other doctors, especially that German bitch, and I don't want anyone else telling me what is appropriate. I want to hear the disposition orders from the Department of Justice, and make sure the processors are doing what they are supposed to do. Nothing else." Bernie concluded, letting a big sigh and wheeze after he was through.

Dr. Amir was quiet, then spoke in a low voice. “The department of corrections wouldn’t allow that. The project was founded under rehabilitation. That includes psychiatric approval.”

“The project is already approved though the Psychiatric Association, I just want to continue to do so. I’ll give reports you can read every few months, but ultimately, I want to control the computer systems myself. No one else.” Bernie stated.

Dr. Amir was quiet.

Bernie was quiet.

There was a hum from the electronic equipment in the room, and during this silence the air conditioner turned on for a moment and then stopped.

Bernie added, “Otherwise I quit.”

Dr. Amir sat back in his chair and toyed with a pen on his desk. “Do you realize that you would be essentially taking control of the entire facility?”

Bernie nodded, “…Essentially, the computer systems are the facility. Yes.”

“And do you realize, that if something goes wrong, you will be held responsible…?”

“Well, seeing how you handle things when they go wrong, I can’t be worse at it…” Bernie chuckled, “besides, I’m not the CEO, or President, or anything. I’m just an IT guy. You’ll still have to answer to the DOJ, the government, the high council and everything above them.”

“Then no, Bernard. You can’t have control of the entire facility.” Dr. Amir said, shifting in his chair. “It’s an insane idea. You can’t just demand private access to the work of thousands.”

Bernie leaned back in his chair this time, quietly sighing and wheezing simultaneously. “Well, I can’t stay here otherwise. I can’t ensure the safety of our two pets. And I can’t be part of this program while we have those two here.”

Dr. Amir replied, “So this is about them, not some power fantasy?”

“Oh, don’t get me wrong, It’s also about a power fantasy. I definitely want to push you out of the power spot, and take, essentially, everyone’s job; the important part anyway. But technically speaking, I can’t ensure that certain documents don’t leak about a certain pair of clones in a certain level five secure facility, who were supposed to be released in about 48 real time hours.” Bernie wheezed. “I think that might be your first concern.”

Dr. Amir smiled. “Do you really think people are going to care that much?”

Bernie’s face stiffened at Dr. Amir’s new tone. “They should care.”

“Yes, but they won’t. Two clones sentenced to Paris indefinitely. Who will really care?” Dr. Amir stated.

“They aren’t just two clones. They’re people. They’re… siblings, you know that.”

“But no one else does. And even if you tell them, it’s a tabloid story. Everyone is scared of big government. Everyone knows Paris is a place where sometimes people disappear. Everyone knows it’s a big scary box where bad people go in, and good people come out. It’s association. If two people go in, it’s because they were bad. And if they don’t come out, it’s because it’s not their time yet. Society will continue forward. No one will bat an eye for clones. Heck. I bet most will assume you got your data wrong."

"I never get my data wrong." Bernie stated, standing up. "I'll go straight to the police then, and see what they have to say." Bernie knew this was an empty threat. The police were clearly under the payroll of the DOJ, and the DOJ along with the DOC were under the advisement of the Paris program central computer. Now that the city's main files were also under Paris, whatever the Paris files said superseded everything else. Paris was the main file facility of the entire city, the ultimate vault of information.

"Bernie. I know it's difficult for you, but sit down. Take a week off, and come back fresh, okay? Think about it. You don't really want to leave what you've worked so hard on. And you don't want to make trouble for Paris…" Dr. Amir softened his tone.

Bernie paused and looked around the room, thinking.

"Let's say you did succeed. And everyone rose against Paris. Let's say there are riots and the government wanted to shut down the place. How would that play out? The first fundamental systems we produced were security. There is no escape from Paris. We even built the consequential system to be baseline, not externally stimulated. No matter what an outside party does, if they remove a resident from Paris before they're discharged, the resident will die. Plain and simple. We wrote that in together, remember? There's no chance this ends well for any resident, especially the innocent girl, or the rehabilitated brother of hers. Think about it."

Bernie stood there, then nodded slowly. Dr. Amir felt that he had reached Bernie, and waved his hand. "Take off for a week. Feel better, then come back in. We'll discuss making the facility more comfortable for all the residents, including our 'pets' as you called them." Bernie turned away and left the office.

As he closed the door, he sprinted to the elevator to reach the control room as fast as he could. Dr. Amir turned his computer on and closed a letter of resignation for the DownTown Press and accessed the security files. Bernie reached the elevator, and smashed the third-floor control room button as hard as he could. He tapped his foot as the elevator responded. Dr. Amir opened security personnel files and found Bernie's access files and scrolled down the extensive lists. Bernie reached the third floor and ran to the control room door and grabbed his badge. Dr. Amir deselected the control room door and other access points along the third floor and removed Bernie's access. Bernie held his badge to the door but the door remained locked. Bernie tried it again, and again. He typed out the emergency code on the door's keypad, but to no avail. Dr. Amir closed the security files. "Go home Bernie." He said to himself, and returned to the resignation letter, the final loose end. Bernie sat in the hallway, wheezing. "Fuck you, doc."

Ally told Shakeem the story, and some of the other boys stayed to listen. It was the first time, in a long time, they heard a female voice that wasn't computerized. Something about being told a story around armchairs near a glowing television made the boys feel cozy. Some forgot where they were and almost were delivered consequences for getting too close to each other. Some were content to just look at the new resident, the female form, art within itself, no commentary needed. But as Ally told the story, parts of it Shakeem wished she kept to herself. He didn't need to know how sad she was, or how dangerous it was sneaking around to get information. There were agents that could have arrested her for just thinking about breaking into a secure facility like this one. Bribing an official for an exclusive press pass when her boss wouldn't spring for one, and finally ending up in prison seemed to be a story of failure, not success. However, the other boys were impressed, and his sister seemed satisfied with herself, at least for now.

"When do we speak to the treatment specialists? I know they're the only human contact we get from the outside world. They'll be able to set everything right." Ally asked.

"I see mine on Wednesdays!" one of the younger boys offered, failing to understand the true question.

"Thursday for me!" another boy followed suit.

"Every two weeks, since my last fight…" another boy mumbled, still regretting trying to swing on another resident.

"I saw mine two weeks ago, just about… But there's something I have to tell you," Shakeem started. Ally looked at him in an inviting way, "Yeah? Go on then…"

"I think this was an awful idea. My treatment specialist told me I'd be out in two weeks, that was 12 days ago." Shakeem uttered.

"Yeah… but they keep changing the dates. They never let you out when they were supposed to, remember?" Ally stated confidently.

"Yes, but they said there was a new system that decided I could leave in two days. A new processor or something decided it was time." Shakeem hesitated, "I think you wasted your time."

Ally thought for a moment. There was nothing in the brochures and nothing in the files she got from the city about any new processors. There were some dealings with the City and Automation that seemed to be making headlines, but that always happens in tech circles whenever they can stuff more RAM into a smaller hole. But still… what was her brother talking about? Maybe this time the computer would have let him out. Maybe it really was stupid to get herself this close to this machine. "Well, regardless, once the treatment specialist I'm assigned to sees I have no disposition order, and notices I'm not even charged with anything, they'll have to let me out. It's just a matter of time really." Ally said, with confidence to cheer up her brother.

Shakeem nodded, as the collars lit up with their respective lights, and it was time for A and C pods to return to their rooms, just as D and B pods returned from the gym through the cluster doors. Every resident shuffled back to their rooms, silently. Shakeem wanted to hug his sister. Every resident in the building wanted to hug his sister. But he knew he couldn't. Not even because of the consequences he would get, but because of the intellectual task he had to focus on. He had to make sure he was released on time. If the computer truly did make a mistake, and Ally was here by a glitch, there was a chance she wouldn't even have a treatment specialist. It was up to him to make sure he saw his, and explained to her what was going on.

4495 moved in sync with the others toward her pod, and then her room. She wanted to reach out to her brother, but ultimately could not. She, of course, didn't want to embarrass him or anything, but more than anything she wanted to spare him another second of those debilitating shocks. She knew they were nanobots, and she knew the collars controlled them, but more than anything she wanted to spare him from having to experience the pain of this building for one more second. What else could she do now but wait? She reached her room and sat quietly. The overhead speakers chimed, and stated good night. The lights went off. Aaliyah teared up just a little bit as she thought about what he had said. Maybe this was a mistake. Maybe she could have done more outside of the facility. Protesting, going to rallies, trying to appeal to government, all of those things had failed. What else could she do now? Her stomach grew a pit, and she felt her heart sink into it. Part of her, she realized, had given up. Part of her didn't want to fight anymore. Part of her didn't care where they lived. She sniffled. She just wanted to be with her brother again.

Ally woke up late, as usual, and rushed out of bed. She almost hit her head on the underside of the top bunk, which was full of clothes and papers and books. She shoveled spoonfuls of cereal into her mouth in between sliding on her pants and shirt and skipping clearing the dishes in order to sprint down the apartment steps to the street. The various people she would meet on the stairwell would each individually tell her that the elevator was broken again, and she would nod, or grunt, or pant, "Okay! Thanks!" before continuing down the stairs as fast as she could.

Once on the street, the hustle of the day had already started in full swing. People were everywhere in this part of the city, and the only vehicles on the road were very simple auto-rides from companies picking up their employees and public transports. Most of them were full already, but Ally had to squeeze herself onto one that had at least one spot left, or at worst, had a compromised vacancy counter. Some sensors wouldn't pick up a small child, or even a limber kid if they snuck on the bus. It happened, but not enough to raise much of a concern, but that also meant one more spot for a late person like Ally on an already full vehicle. Public transports were designed to be automatic and self-cleaning. Because the city was designed on a grid-like pattern, every road that ran north to south had a certain number of transports that made stops at every 4 blocks, and other transports ran east to west doing the same. You could grab any transport going in any direction and wind up within 4 blocks of your destination, eventually. Ally didn't need to sit and wait for two hours for the transport to make its way through the entire city, she needed to find the specific bus that would put her just 2 blocks from the grocer, her second new job.

She found the bus, and luckily it wasn't completely full yet. She got onto the bus and paid her fee with a pass, and mentally calculated how much she'd have left in her account. She found a seat near the center of the bus next to another young woman around her age. They exchanged looks of exaggerated exhaustion and smiled, then quietly went back into their own thoughts.

"If I work at the grocer from 7am to 3pm, I can head to the record hall before they close at 5, then I can edit that story and submit to Editor Eddy before he leaves the office at 9pm. Then I can sleep a bit earlier for tomorrow and hopefully not be late…" she thought to herself. Editor Eddy considered himself a nice guy; even if he didn't get a chance to read the work, if you submitted it to him before 9pm, even down to the second on deadline day, he'd consider it on time. That gave *him* one less day to actually edit the work for his own deadlines, but he recognized that most reporters had second jobs, and most were busy and working out of homes, not offices like he was. He had a heart. Ally was grateful for that, and used the courtesy frequently.

The transport stopped at the designated spot, and the woman next to Ally slid by her to exit. They exchanged another socially acceptable glance and Ally moved over to take her seat, by the window. The move was instinctual, but regrettable as soon as she made the switch. The seat was warm, and thus uncomfortable, as Ally for a moment thought about this stranger's behind for a few moments, but soon those thoughts subsided. She looked across the streets as she passed them, the humming of the bus's motor as she moved along. Her stomach digested few bites of cereal, and politely asked for more in a stern growl. She sighed, and thought about James. He would be next to her right now, she thought to herself. She wouldn't be looking out the window, but instead talking to him about school and maybe a test he had to study for. Maybe she could even be quizzing him. Maybe he would get one wrong, and she would know the answer, and she could show him how to find the right answer himself. She smiled sadly at the thought of his face lighting up as he got the answer on his own, and continued to answer question after question correctly. She daydreamed about him coming home after school, to their nice house outside the city on a cool Autumn day showing off his perfect test grades. She would be sitting in the living room, working on a painting she was going to submit to an art fair, or festival, and she would put down her brush and tools to go celebrate his success. And then the transport stopped. It was a break down.

Sometimes the public transports broke down in the middle of the commute, but another one was already on its way. The systems in the transport were sensitive to safety, so sometimes there isn't even anything wrong with them. The transports could think there "might" be something wrong, and shut itself down for maintenance after calling for another transport to take its place on the route. Some bad-actors have used this to their advantage and purposefully smashed a window, or broke a headlight just see a hundred people or so miss a few minutes out of their day, knowing the transport would recognize a structural flaw and shut down for maintenance. Ally had to reconfigure.

"Damn. Okay… bus should get here in a few minutes, but the delay means I won't be able to clock in right at 8, so maybe more like 8:15 which means I'll start earning real cash at around 8:30, and then maybe I'll have to do some extra work for Eddy over the weekend to break even…." She thought to herself as the rest of the transport groaned and complained. Luckily it was only a few moments before the next transport arrived and the automated voice instructed the passengers to board the following transport to continue on the same stops as before. Ally quickly did so, hopefully able to get a fresh seat, and hopefully near the front of the transport to get out quicker so she could sprint to the grocer.

When she arrived, she signed in with her fingerprint at 8:07am, still too late to be considered for the 8:00am pay cycle. This grocer was one of the last in the city to not be 100% automated. The owner couldn't afford the machine that moved product from the transportation trucks to the vendor machines. The trick was, for the machine, fitting each item into the exact slot perfectly, especially when it came to slightly oblong or misshapen products like vegetables or new promotions. The update software was such that an older model would not be compatible with the mechanics of the robotic arm; both had to be state of the art, not a reused model. The owner didn't have the money yet to make such a change, so in the meantime he hired day laborers to show up and help out. Ally applied to work as much as she could in the morning to supplement her financial plans. She would arrive, clock in as early as she could, and start the mind-numbing work of moving boxes and crates and single items literally from one side of the warehouse to the other side of the warehouse, where another person would place the items in the correct slots. Sometimes Ally would switch with her partner and she would be the one to place the items in the correct slots. Ally and her partner might take breaks now and then and switch off, but for most of the day it was her and whoever she was paired with for those hours, just physically moving stuff around. It wasn't hard, and the items were rarely heavy or laborious. It gave Ally time to daydream and think.

After her shift she caught the next transport to the Hall of Records. Sometimes she would go here for information for a story, or she would need to cross reference a source, or even sometimes on errands for Eddy. Most things you could do over a computer over the internet systems, but certain information wasn't uploaded correctly, or easily found. Very old files might not be uploaded at all, and some files were purposefully redacted or censored on the internet. Sometimes only certain authorizations could access the files online due to hackers and people misusing or corrupting the information. Searching information in the Hall of Records was a more direct way to get the information needed without the hassle of combing through websites or circumventing other hurdles. Ally walked through the grand arches she was familiar with, and much like a library she tried to stay quiet. She found an information kiosk and started queries about Paris Youth Correctional Facility. She looked through articles by previous colleagues and resulted in nothing. She found testimonials by previous inmates and how the program was difficult, but important for them to learn how to behave. Most, if not all, entries were positive. Most residents stated their success or failure was due to their treatment specialist, and that the time at Paris was a time away from everything to rethink their mistakes, to avoid negative consequences, and to focus on the positive parts of life. Ally thought about her brother, and if James would say similar things.

Ally would periodically receive mail from the Department of Corrections about her brother. They would be updates on sentencing mostly. At first it was a few months, then it was a year, then a few more months, than a few more months after that. Many times, she wrote back demanding an explanation to why her brother was locked up longer than the sentence required. Many times, she rushed into offices unannounced to get a word from a politician, or anyone who would be able to answer her questions, and almost always she was turned away by security and turned away from the office entirely. She would receive letters giving her, essentially, an advertisement for Paris, stating how great the facility is, and how rehabilitated all those who enter feel after they exit.

Ally grew suspicious that this was more of a brainwashing facility than anything else. How can you change a person so drastically like this? How can you turn someone from a cold-blooded killer, for example, into a model citizen in just a few months? She did believe people could change, sure, but from a nearly fully automated facility? Like her grocery store? A place as cold and unfeeling as that could offer changes that are lasting to the human spirit, and soul? She continued reading until she found a few more leads.

"Some State Paris Is Not What It Seems", read the article headline. As usual, the author of the story was a discredited reporter who apparently faked their data or made up their sources. She scrolled through the article and it hit most of the same points she had seen before. "My son is a zombie!", she kept scrolling, "He was extended 8 times!", more scrolling, "Is Paris What is seems? You decide", the report ended. Nothing of substance, just hearsay and opinions.

Next article. A new one, only from a few months ago. "City Plans to Integrate Files", the title said. Ally thought this had little to do with Paris as a facility. She continued to skim the article. "Drivers of the 64Set will be processed at three times the speed of the normal 12Set, giving the city ample space to integrate law enforcement profiles against that of other cities…" the article droned on. This wasn't about Paris; this was about the city offloading their data to private companies again. This had been going on for a while. Private companies would roll into a city, start off small, pay taxes like normal, but then end up requiring more and more city resources such as power and space. Soon jobs would be siphoned to the company and the city government would be reliant on them for their economy, soon the city wouldn't have enough man-power or economic power to bully the company, and the company would effectively own the city. Soon, if the company was a tech company, or a robotics company, the innovation would begin, and the city would be outfitted with auto-rides, and automated businesses. The city would have no choice to accept the help and improve the economy overall. The city and some private company would exist together, a symbiosis of sorts. In her city it as PsyClone who won the war over the city's heart, beating NeuroRex just slightly in health and services. NeuroRex had many other cities under control across the country, and PsyClone had just outfoxed them with some newer breakthroughs with cloning and healthcare.

Ally never really thought about the details of cloning or what the ethics would be. She thought there were a bit too many people already. With automation running the world, people had to figure out what to do with themselves. Items were cheap, but human services were expensive. Because it didn't cost too much to buy food or food items anymore, and since owners didn't have to pay any people to work their stores outside of a mechanic once or twice a month, all the money it would have spent on those workers went to the mechanic or any other human elements. Or, at least most of it. Instead of having taxi drivers and bus drivers anymore, the only human interaction was with the mechanic or the inspectors. It was the same with medicine as well, many nurses were laid off when human services programming was upgraded and installed through PsyClone, and implanted into NeuroRex hardware. Since one could be retrofitted to fit the other, it ended up being that a Health Services Machine could administer medication, create providential diagnosis, and then write up a report for the most likely effective course of action for the patient. The only issue was that many patients felt that machines to be cold and unfeeling. PsyClone arrived and provided cloned nurse entities from human nurses. They could record the neurological processes of thousands of nurses, combine them all into the most caring, kind, and warmhearted messages and tones, and deliver the cold-logical and factual data from NeuroRex with a dignified, helpful and warm human touch. People were delighted. Nurses became obsolete. Now and then a doctor would be necessary to oversee and check abnormalities if the health service machine requested it, but more likely than not, the doctor signed off on the recommendation and went back to do his or her own research. The things only human beings could do gained the most respect and gained the most influence or wealth. No longer was artistry just a poor man's fantasy, it was lucrative. Different styles of art and passion projects were the base of the economy in a certain sense. Some were known to even trade paintings and stories, and poems in their own form of currency, in certain circles.

Ally read the article, more bored than anything. There was nothing here about integrating files that she could use to learn more about the program, and possibly make sense of the systems at hand. She was determined to see for herself what the facility was like, and certain that she might have found an avenue to get there. Something caught her attention in the article. More information about the integration will be explained at a Town Hall meeting, in just a few months' time. She would be able to go there, maybe with a press pass, and ask her questions. If lucky, even get to go on a tour. She would do whatever she had to do get that press pass. She made plans to meet with Eddy and maybe the chief editor the next time she was near the office. She had to get this to work.

Ally printed the article for a few cents and walked out of the Hall of Records and caught a public transport back to her apartment. While on the transport she felt her phone vibrate in her pocket. She had cut out many of the services that were costly: live video was extra, GPS tracking was extra, and other apps and videos were extra. The phone itself was practically free, but every other service was individualized, this saved money, and Ally needed all she could get. She slid the phone out of her pocket and opened her bank account to see a deposit from the work earlier today. The turnaround was good enough, she thought, as she put the phone back into her pocket and did more calculations. If at this rate she could keep up her grocer job, while still getting at least one article out a week, she would be able to afford a lawyer. Once she had enough information to cast doubt on Paris, and once she had a source or something to show that Paris wasn't all it was meant to be, she could hire a lawyer to do more investigating and bring charges against the facility. They could look at the letters the DOC was sending her, and make some claim about the violation of fair and usual punishments. Her brother was sentenced, but they changed the sentence afterward for no apparent reason than that a robot told them to. This couldn't be legal, right? She asked herself, still swimming in mental doubt. If all goes well, she would have enough money after the town hall. By then, she would have everything she needed; everything other than an inside look to seal the deal.

Ally walked into the lobby of her apartment and swiped her payment card to pay for rent at the kiosk there. She never met the owner of the apartment, and technically never would. Her room was rented from others who had rented a larger portion of the rooms already. This was further broken down and owners were often changing hands. Luckily, the owners often changed hands automatically as the market shifted, meaning Ally didn't have to change much of her behavior. To pay she would type in her apartment number, the prompt would show who owned it and what the price for that room was. She would pay for a few days to weeks at a time with her money card. The key would remain active and she could still have access to her room. If she were to miss a payment, there would be a 'Vacancy' label instead of "In Use", and technically anyone else could purchase the room from under her. It was up to her to make sure the room stayed payed for. Because it was automatic, and the owners changed so quickly from month to month, it would take weeks to get an appeal or access into a locked room to remove one's stuff. There was an option to get into a vacant room for a reduced price for half a day or for a few hours, but that option seemed to also be dependent on how long the room had been in use for previously, and how long it had been vacant since then. The building's automated room checking system would begin clearing entities from a room and sanitizing the space after a few days of a new vacancy, all with the use of machines and robots. There were a few close calls for Ally, missing a payment here or there. She and her brother had to wait in the lobby for a few hours once until her payment card was updated for the day's work, and finally, late into the night, or early into the morning, they were able to rest together on their bunk beds. Ally whispered an apology as they lay in the darkness that night, but James never heard it; he was already asleep.

Ally entered her apartment and set down her personal groceries and her bag. The apartment was small and a bit cramped for her style; she wanted a large area to look out and see the sky, and maybe a lounging area to relax and just breathe in. Instead, she had small kitchen area with one counter that seemed to be connected to the side of the refrigerator, and a sink. She did have a small living space area, enough for an old couch a neighbor was trying to get rid of. "Instead of dragging that down the steps, I can take it for you," she said to the neighbor who was moving out. James helped her move it when he got home, and after some cleaning, the apartment and the couch wasn't in bad shape. James and Ally would sit on the couch after school, and before Ally worked sometimes and talk. She would tease him about his studies and sometimes his friends, and he would retort and laugh at her stories. They'd watch movies sometimes if Ally got home early enough. They liked to make up alternate story lines from other character's point of view. In a romantic comedy, James would take the point of view of the ex-boyfriend who was pushed aside for the main character. In a horror movie, Ally would take the point of view of a random neighbor who just heard screaming all night and ignored it. They would add their own commentary and giggle as the story lined up or deviated wildly from their improv. The couch held that laughter, that warmth, and that love.

She didn't sit on it anymore.

She disrobed from the clothes she wore and quickly used the shower. The warm water felt nice as she slowly turned up the heat every few minutes, hot, hotter, hotter. Once she felt completely clean, she wrapped herself in towels and dried her hair as best she could before she turned on her home computer. She placed the articles she received from the Hall of Records on the top bunk of the bed after highlighting important information, and sat on a chair in the kitchen, looking over at the small window in the wall behind the couch. The night fell faster than she thought it would, and she checked the time. She worked for a few hours, and just barely made the deadline. In addition to the article, she sent a request for the press pass.

She closed her computer and laid back on her bottom bunk, looking at the bunk above her.

"Hey…", she said aloud, "I love you, you know?"

The silence clawed a hole in her chest and sat there, sinking into her stomach.

Bernie was sitting down across from the FBI agent and sipped from a disposable cup of black coffee. The room wasn't cozy, but Bernie didn't feel intimidated. There was a table between them, metallic and reflecting the overhead lights. On top of the table sat a recording device and a few papers, notepad, pens, another mug of coffee. Behind the agent was a one-way window with a reflective tint. The FBI agent said his name was Carter, and that he was skeptical of the entire process at Paris. Carter didn't believe in 'rehabilitation' in these new fancy mechanisms sweeping the country. He liked things old school, he told Bernie. They had been talking for a few hours now, taking short breaks as Carter talked to colleagues and offering Bernie food and drink for his testimony.

Bernie put down his cup of coffee and wheezed, "So you wanna know more about the place or not? You don't have to believe it, but that's how it all works."

"Let's say everything you're saying is true, that these collars and nano boys, or bots, or bytes, or whatever are controlling these kids, so what?" Carter played the 'What's this guy's real intention' card.

"First of all, it's nanobots, and that's very important that you understand we're talking about state of the art, private sector, not allowed to civilians, sort of thing. These aren't the basic tracker bots you get from HQ, or what a standard employee gets from work. We're talking biometric next level tech." He wheezed as Carter looked unimpressed,

"Second of all, that was all just background so you understood that this place has a history. What you see in the news isn't all there is, this place has secrets that I can't tell you all about right now. Secrets I want you all to do a real investigation into…" Bernie trailed off, partly to convey his seriousness, and partly to add some mystery. To Bernie, this was like selling an idea, rather than trying to begin an investigation. Bernie also thought Carter was stupid, a dinosaur left-over from the previous age. Carter didn't understand the nuance or the elegance of a perfectly formatted file, or a compression mechanism that operated at maximum efficiency. Carter was probably an idiot with a gun and a sense of intuition that got him into the FBI. Bernie quickly started losing respect for Carter when he asked if messing with time was torture for the residents, or when he couldn't understand what conditioning was, or why mice would be pressing buttons to get food. In response, Bernie grew more and more lighthearted, laughing at his ignorance, playing off the idea of an expert. While it was fun for Bernie to talk to someone who was so completely in the dark about how the facility operated, it was also time consuming. It was wasting time that Bernie did not have, he only had a few more days until he was expected back at Paris himself.

"We aren't really interested in Paris," Carter said after Bernie stopped talking again, "whatever secrets they have fall under the Department of Justice for that district, and we don't care much to interfere with that." When Carter saw Bernie's face change into disappointment, and maybe even regret, he added, "We do need and appreciate all information, of course, especially from private organizations using high tech innovations on human beings, but Paris Youth Correctional isn't really the private organization using high tech innovations on human beings that we're interested in. We're more concerned about the parent company, PsyClone."

"PsyClone?" Bernie stated, "Parent company? That's not right."

"We have it under authority that the two organizations have been intertwined for quite some time, and that PsyClone has recently been pulling the strings at Paris. We also have it under investigation for numerous human rights violations and human cloning practices that are currently under legal restriction. We also know that you personally have worked with head researchers there, and designed some of their processing capabilities."

"I… I didn't…" Bernie was not used to having the tables turn on him this quickly, and it felt like he was back in Dr. Amir's office, being told that he wasn't allowed at the big boy's table. "When did this start?"

"That isn't important Mr. Douglas. What is important is whatever you can tell me about how to access the server data for PsyClone. We know they routed much of their data into Paris, but those files were ancillary and for their public front. PsyClone the business is transparent, but we're interested in PsyClone the research facility; they're doing special operations in there and we need to know what they are." Carter stated this as if he had explained it to twenty other people before Bernie. These were merely facts to Carter, and Bernie could accept them or not. Bernie was still putting it all together from his point of view. If he was working for PsyClone this whole time, did Dr. Amir, or Dr. Chanel? Who else knew about the merger, and what did this mean for Bernie?

"Mr. Douglas?" Carter asked, after a long moment of silence.

"I… I think I should go." Bernie said instinctively. If he wasn't in control of what information existed, his first instinct was to escape. He was not in control, and never was. He was part of a larger game, a mere paint stroke in an elaborate mosaic. He was starting to get the picture now.

"Well, hold on…" Carter stiffened up, "We know you know something, you worked there and you know about secrets. We know Paris holds residents and all, but we need to know about anything suspicious going on at PsyClone, whether it is data related or tech related, or even human related. Can we count on you to keep us informed?" Carter held out a card with a handwritten number on the back of it. Bernie looked at the card while he collected his papers and shoved them back into his folders. This was not supposed to happen like this at all, Bernie thought. He was supposed to walk in, like a savvy spy from an old movie, and offer information. Information was money to FBI agents, right? And he thought he had so much of it. He was a millionaire in information, and he wanted to spend it all in the right place. He would douse this pathetic FBI agent, and his fellow agents behind that glass window in his technological cash flow, and drown them in how intricate and specific the Paris program was. He would talk about his central processor, and when they ooed and awed at how amazing the processor was, he'd talk about how he designed it and get them to worship at his feet. Maybe they'd offer him a job, maybe they'd just be so grateful Bernie showed up and did such a good deed. He'd be forever immortalized as a saint. He would give them the information on what Dr. Amir was doing to those two kids, and the FBI would be able to demand access to the DOJ and DOC files and have Bernie replace the backup files he kept on his personal drives. After that, and once Dr. Amir was arrested for essentially attempted murder, Bernie would be put in charge of operations. He fantasized about seeing a collar around Dr. Amir's neck.

But, no. The FBI didn't give a shit about Paris and its processors. The agents behind the window probably were bored out of their mind hearing about psychology and nanobots and brain scans from Bernie. They were billionaires with information, and Bernie's pathetic million dollars was running out the more Bernie spoke. If PsyClone was really under the FBI's radar, then the CIA might be next, and if Bernie wasn't careful either operation could want the entire project destroyed or carted off to a black ops site. Bernie could be shipped off to be interrogated, not on his own terms. Bernie could even find himself liable if anyone wanted to make heads roll. Dr. Amir might be taken down, sure, but so would everyone working for him too. If PsyClone was under fire, clearly everything and everyone working under them could be too.

Bernie wheezed in a raspy, thick manner as he thought about this. Carter offered him water. Bernie declined. "It was nice.... Speaking... to you," Bernie wheezed as he stood up. Carter stood up too, looking a bit concerned, but still extending his card to Bernie.

"If there's anything you find that's interesting, let us know." Carter instructed Bernie. Bernie nodded quickly, swallowed, took the card, and reached for the door to leave. Carter turned toward the mirrored window and nodded, then followed Bernie out the room, and out of the building.

Shakeem sat in class and didn't pay attention to a single word. It had been a few days, since Ally showed up, and she had been doing fine to avoid consequences and gain some respect among the other residents. Shakeem noticed that the boys stopped making sexual comments, overall, and saw her more like an older sister the way he did. He absentmindedly wrote out the algebraic formula the simulated teacher explained, and looked around the room. Shawn didn't sit next to him anymore, but was in the corner next to Frank. They weren't talking, but instead writing notes to each other. It looked enough like academic notes that the cameras must not have registered it. Shakeem noticed that Shawn was particularly good at learning the thresholds for certain consequences, or at least getting Frank to exhibit them.

Shakeem was distracted not by Shawn, or his sister really, but instead that he was still here. His treatment specialist hadn't shown up for him, and he was not called into the treatment room for some time now. Karah was usually on time for his appointments, and while he didn't like her particularly, and he didn't think she knew what she was doing, it wasn't like her to cancel appointments. For the first time in a year, he actually had something he wanted to tell her. He actually had news to share with his outside contact, and she disappears. After all that talk about him doing so well, and that he could be released soon, she just stops showing up? Maybe she quit. Sometimes that happens, and the resident will get a new specialist in a few days or a few weeks depending on the availability. Treatment Specialist at Paris was an extremely well-paid job, and extremely sought after, so most residents didn't have to wait long to be assigned someone after an old one quit.

Despite all of this, Shakeem was not selected for treatment time, day after day. During treatment time for the other residents on the schedule, Shakeem and the other kids not on the roster had extra recreation time or free time. Sometimes reflection time was used as well, meaning stay in one's room and think, or sleep, or read. Even still, it was a painful reminder that you were stuck while other people got a glimpse of outside. For Shakeem, it wasn't as bad, since he was able to hear about the outside world from a primary source. Every day, for some activity or another, his pod would be paired with A-pod and he would be able to talk to his sister. They couldn't touch, or hug, or cuddle as they used to on their couch in their comfortable, warm, living room, and they couldn't watch the movies they used to, or even chat before bed anymore. But Shakeem could sit next to her in recreation, or pass a ball back and forth with her, or even sit next to her in free time and watch an outdated TV show. That was enough for him at the moment.

While he hated the idea of his sister being here, and hated the fact that they were both locked up because of his stupid decisions. He also didn't mind being in the facility as much. Whereas before he was annoyed at his peers, and remained quiet and out of the way in order to squeeze by out of the program and get back home. He realized he only wanted to return home to see his sister again. He wanted to apologize for leaving her and hanging with his stupid friends and promise her that he would spend every chance he could at home with her. He wanted to get a job and provide food and contribute to the little family they had. He just wanted to make her life easier.

At the moment she was in there with him. If he did get out, and she didn't, he would be in the exact same position she was. If his treatment specialist did show up and did move toward termination and completion of his rehabilitation, he would be able to return to his own life, and with his completion of the program, probably get first pick in some good jobs here and there, but he would also be without his sister. He'd be in the same situation she was, using every un-busy moment thinking about her and longing for her to return. He felt such a connection to her that he felt completely whole, now, knowing where she was, and that she was safe.

Say what you want about Paris, he thought, but he was always safe here. He thought about the new intakes, always wanting to prove they're the 'baddest' or that they could beat up anyone, or that they are the top of the food chain. He could imagine new intakes trying that with his sister and how tempted he would be to beat their faces in. He was comforted by the idea that the cameras and the facility staff would intervene beforehand, and that no one could touch her, not even himself. At least in here, we're both safe, he concluded his thought. His collar lit up, and he followed the line to the cafeteria for lunch.

Ally finished her lunch as the boys on her pod asked her if she wanted any of their food. She politely declined, as she always did. She didn't want to 'owe' anyone anything, and she didn't want to seem like she was playing favorites to anyone in particular. She wanted to remain as neutral as possible. Hopefully she would become invisible after a while and the residents would leave her be. This seemed to be impossible for her, she noticed; the boys were changing around her. For every one of the crass things the boys would say, there would be just as many or more sweet and sensitive things the boys would say. Many of them took up the practice of cutting before her in line, to make sure she was last. At first, she thought she was being hazed or something, but she overheard,

"… So make sure you beat her to the line each time. She's usually kind of slow so it isn't hard."

"Yeah, but why?"

"Dummy, be a gentleman! This way no one can stare at her ass in the hallway!"

"Ohhh… But usually *women* go first."

"Not anymore."

"Oh, okay. I get it."

"Yeah, and if you do look at her ass for too long, we won't play with you at rec either."

"I get it, I get it. I won't look!"

"Good,"

In their own way, they were trying to be men. Ally could appreciate that. Ally first appreciated that a few boys on her pod would also hold up a towel in front of them when she showered in the morning as well, keeping the other boys from being able to see if she were to remove all of her clothing. She typically did not do so, but in changing her clothes and using her towels to stay as clothed as possible, she greatly appreciated the gesture.

She lined up as lunch ended, and in standing at the back of the line, the residents moved quietly back to the cluster, passing Shakeem's group. Shakeem became something of a celebrity as well, Ally noticed. Many times, Shakeem was swarmed with residents before she arrived to meet him, many, she overheard, asking him personal questions about his life, and what he and she did together. She was sure he didn't enjoy that sort of attention, but at least the mob of residents left them alone when they were together. They would clear the way for either Shakeem or Ally to meet each other, then the two would, almost in synchronicity, sit down, begin walking together, or play a game. There was never any moment of awkward silence, or pausing in their conversation. It was a comfortable, calm conversation full of smiles, laughter, and what some might recognize as love.

Bernie arrived back in the facility and was greeted by Dr. Amir and two-armed security guards. Dr. Amir walked with Bernie through the hallways and to the control room, but continued to walk pass the door to another room down the hall.

"Welcome back, Bernie." Dr. Amir said with a smile. "I hope you had some time to clear your head."

"I think I did," Bernie said, trying to sound convincing. In truth he had spent many hours traveling to the intelligence bureau station and after waiting for a meeting and filling out forms, and traveling more, he was still sleep deprived and frustrated at the entire situation. "I have found a new perspective," he wheezed as they walked past his old door. "What is this?" Bernie asked as they stopped at the new door down the hallway.

"This is you." Dr. Amir stated. "This is your new station. Try your badge." The security officer gave Bernie his badge, and Bernie tried it on the door. The light flickered green and unlocked. Bernie stepped inside as the two guards stood post. Dr. Amir stood in the doorway.

"It's a limited access control system. We have copied the files you had and most of the central processor into a simulator of itself. It took nearly a full week to copy everything, but we got it done just in time. In here you can't make any lasting changes, but you can create new programs and new processes all you'd like." Dr. Amir paused, and let Bernie process it all. "You'll still get error messages from the central processor, but before any changes are to be implemented, they'll come through me."

"Fuck you." Bernie whispered through a wheeze as he looked at a perfectly clean, spotless counter top, three monitors, and a few computers below. No interface modules, no command queries, and no custom hardware from the control room he had personally brought in to make his job more streamlined and to his liking. When Bernie worked his best, he 'slipped into' the computer system in a sense, his muscle memory was tuned that when there was an error, or a ping, his wrist would flick, and his pinky would know which button to push without thought. His screens were color coded to match what he was working on, what he was referencing, and what he was correcting, in a perfect array of colors and code. He now looked at the three lifeless, standard computer screens. He said it again a bit louder, “Fuck you Doc.”

“I hope you like your new station Bernie. I’ll accept your requests for changes after I reviewed them at the end of the week. I know it’ll be a bit slower than you’d like. I know you like to implement fast changes and test them in real time using the central computer as its own simulator, but it’s an awful waste of processor power. So, we’ll do it this way from now on.” Dr. Amir stated, ignoring Bernie’s frustration. “Also, you can’t do any lasting damage to our file systems, or to the residents. I think it’s best that I take care of that from now on.”

“You son of a bitch, you really expect me to sit in here and just hand you protocol slips, and error resolutions like a… like.. like a Wendell? I’m not fucking Wendell; I do my own troubleshooting and cross referencing. I’m the one who fucking build the simulator, how dare you tell me to use it?” Bernie exclaimed. One of the security guards turned around, as Dr. Amir put up his hand to quell him.

“Two guards will be outside your door from now on,” Dr. Amir stated, completely ignoring Bernie, “And you will be escorted by them anywhere within the facility. Back there,” Dr. Amir gestured, “is the sleeping room, bathroom, etc. just like in the other room. We moved your personal belongings back there. You’ll also need clearance from me before you leave the facility.”

“… what? Bef—before I leave? What does that mean? You mean I have to check with you before my two-week stint is over?” Bernie asked.

“No, Bernie,” Dr. Amir turned to leave the room. “It means I have three pets now.” The door closed.

Shawn was quite nervous, actually. He had been messing around with people who weren't quite geniuses and he was afraid he had lost some of his edge. He had been running distractions for bank tellers, talking his way through security guards at the mall, and even law enforcement officers had let him slide when caught red handed. He prided himself over the ability to look innocent and to be taken seriously depending on the peer or superior that was talking to him at the time. He manipulated his mother into believing he couldn't do wrong, and if anyone saw what he was actually capable of, he would probably be able to convince them it was just their imagination or out of context or something. "People only know what you tell them," was Shawn's favorite things to think, along with, "People want to believe what they already know, you just have to help them". Shawn was able to manipulate because he could figure out what people wanted to believe and he gave them permission to do so. He convinced Frank that his theories were correct, and Frank let him do whatever he wanted since then. He knew his mother wanted a sweet innocent nice son, so he allowed her to be convinced of that. Both Frank and his mother were willing to ignore reality for an extremely long amount of time because Shawn gave them permission to; he gave them the evidence they needed to continue believing their comfortable lies.

Shawn frowned now, as he walked out of the cluster and into the hallway. I do have a weakness, he thought to himself. People without a clear goal or a specific core belief, people who were legitimately not looking for anything but accepted reality for what it was; those people were dangerous. If they look at hard facts and accurately understand probability, I could be in deep shit, he concluded.

Often times Shawn would ask rhetorically, "Hey, what's the chances that I *did something terribly, terribly wrong and you didn't know about it,* versus the chances that *this is just all a misunderstanding*?" The idea here was the make it seem like the person he was talking to was too smart to let something like this happen, while at the same time trying to make his innocence the most likely option. Shawn's actual opponents would be the ones to point out that A) They did know about it, they just found out, hence the current conversation, and B) People do terrible things all the time, there isn't a standard of probability associated with someone doing something wrong, and C) the probability of Shawn lying to get out of trouble was high if he had done something terribly, terribly wrong, and therefore adds to the likelihood of it not being a misunderstanding. For people who didn't have their core beliefs to satiate, admitting that Shawn got away with a terrible act and it took them a long time to find out about it wasn't earth shattering. Most people could easily see the flaws in Shawn's rhetorical question, but when the person was emotionally charged or primed with their own internal needs to continue to see reality the way they wanted to, people get stupid. Shawn found this out and exploited it to the maximum effect. But today, he wasn't sure what would happen.

Shawn shuffled through the line with his other residents following a purple line on the ground. He, along with some of his peers on C-pod seemed to also be in the line, but he also saw some of the boys he was in intake with. Shawn knew better than to talk or gesture to them, but he did feel a twinge of comradery in seeing them all together again since the first day at Paris. The doors opened and Shawn saw for the first time the Treatment Pavilion. He had finally been assigned a treatment specialist. He was finally going to see a person from the outside world that was also dedicated to getting him the hell out of this place. Shawn stood where the speakers and the lines told him to, and he waited with everyone else in silence. The collar lights changed and the doors opened. Shawn took steps inside as the door closed behind him.

Shawn looked around. It was a homier room than any other he had seen. There was a couch in the corner, more soft and comfortable than the sterile ones used for free time, and there was a desk, a nice wooden desk. Even in the outside world a wooden desk was rare. Behind the desk was another door that seemed to mesh with the wall and Shawn, for a split second, had a plan to escape. He could try to convince the treatment specialist to take him with him or her. Maybe he could swing the angle that he really was placed in the facility by accident, or without a trial. Wait. No, he thought, the treatment specialist would have documentation that he was supposed to be here. Could he claim abuse? He could quickly punch himself, maybe make some bruises. He looked up at the camera, then remembered that everything was recorded. Damn it, he yelled inside his own head at himself, you weren't thinking this through. You spent all this time fucking around with morons you didn't even prepare for this moment. Shawn was cross with himself, but overall had a backup plan. He would remain silent. It was a power move, for sure, but you can claim anything if you're silent. This was a trick he used when he was sent to psychologists for his acting out early on in school. If he just stayed silent, once he figured out what angle to take, he could then come back and explain away the silence with anything. He could say he was quiet because he was forced not to say anything by a bully. Maybe he just had crippling social anxiety, thus the other person would have to communicate on his behalf. He could just say he didn't trust anyone, and make up reasons why, reasons to suit his needs. He could just act like he was just so, so, so, so sad, and that sadness made him unable to process anything and result in mutism. If he just didn't say shit, then they couldn't be sure of anything, and he might be able to gain some information, just enough to learn the best way to manipulate the situation to his favor.

As he was thinking this through, the door opened. A young woman stepped through the door holding papers and folders and fidgeting with the bracelet around her wrist. She was mumbling to herself what seemed to a schedule or some sort, and stepped right to the desk.

"Hello there! Please have a seat!" she shoveled all the papers onto the desk and barely looked at Shawn. She had a bright cheery disposition, maybe she was a 'life is what you make it' sort of person, Shawn thought. Shawn went ahead and sat down on the chair facing the woman, and the woman sat in a huff. Shawn guessed that her age was around 24, fresh out of college. She might be a 'let's go save the world' type of person, which Shawn could certainly work with.

"Woo! Okay!" the woman said, as if she had completed some amazing task. "It is certainly nice to meet you in person. Looks like you're here for an indefinite stay, and your case has been turned over to the central computer for behavioral analysis." After a brief pause of her reading something on one of her many papers she said, "Ah, and it looks like you've been quite the trouble maker so far!" she smiled and looked up to finally look at Shawn for more than a second. Shawn tried to hold a blank expression; not angry, not off putting, just a blank, 'am I even here?' sort of look, so he could redefine the experience later. The woman smiled at him and made a silly face, one to say, "You know better mister!" the way a condescending babysitter might say to a kid who broke a minor rule. Clearly, she had no true power, and couldn't actually do anything about his misbehavior, but she also couldn't let it go unaddressed, but also, she had to make Shawn comfortable and open up to her, and the result was... well, a silly face.

"Well, we all make mistakes!" she said, again with inappropriate energy, "I think if you just buckle down and do what you should be doing and behave a bit more, you'll be on track to get out of here on time. My job is to make sure you leave at the right time, so don't go making it too hard on me!" She explained as if talking to a child once more.

"What the hell is wrong with this woman," Shawn thought to himself, "She hasn't introduced herself, hasn't even addressed me by my name, isn't aware that I haven't said a word, or that I'm not responding to anything she's talking about. She isn't asking me how I feel or why I've been acting out. Is this lady on drugs?" Shawn's thoughts must've made his face move or twitch because he felt his eyebrows furrow.

"Well, I think we should meet once a week from now on just to check in and talk. Let me know if you think you need any counseling or to vent, I can offer a bit of privacy if it's super important, but other than that I'll check in with you about your case and any updates or behavior changes you should think about. So far, just stop getting consequences or your stay will be longer! Oh! And also, stop trying to test the consequence system, apparently, you're making everyone's stays longer too! That's no good!" She said, again with a bright overly wide smile and in a high-pitched sing-songy voice that one might use for babies and cute pets.

Shawn had questions. He wasn't sure if his silence tactic was going to work at all. He realized that she was what he feared. She had no real motives. Most counselors and therapists have a great weakness themselves; they actually want to help you. They want you to say they did a good job, and that your life is better. They have a great interest in making sure you're happy with therapy, and that your experience is a positive one. Because of that, you can tell them that you don't like the lights, or the air is too humid, or that you need a cool drink, and they'll bend over backward to make the environment to your liking. The goals of this treatment specialist were unclear. "She said she wants me out on time, but her demeanor suggests she doesn't truly care," he quickly considered. "She didn't ask about my consequences or the events involved, which means she trusts that she knows all the correct information. She doesn't need anyone to confirm her suspicions or her hunches, she's securely convinced that what she read, or what she's convinced of, is true… She can't be manipulated with facts," Shawn had to conclude. Shawn started to sweat as the woman shuffled through and looked over her papers, as if checking if she missed anything. Shawn had to say something, but he drew a blank.

"Well, I think this was a productive session Shawn!" She said, finally stating his name. Until this point, she could have been talking to any other resident, in fact it felt like she was. But when she said his name,

Shawn felt a ripple down his throat, and a tingle in his stomach. It was without thinking, but a word fell out of his mouth.

"..Mom.." Shawn mumbled.

"Oh!", the woman exclaimed, "Yes! I got an update from your mother, and as soon as you're cleared for letters, I'll be bringing those to you as well! If you get some commissary points you can get some paper and writing utensils delivered to your room and you can even write a letter back! Wouldn't that be nice?" Again, the woman stated as if the concept of mail was a foreign concept to Shawn.

"Commissary… I haven't got the points to…" Shawn started without realizing it. The thought of his mother again seemed to have triggered words without thinking. He quickly tried to sober himself up, to stop thinking about things that made him emotional. He had to figure this woman out before she left, not ask silly questions he already knew the basic responses to.

"Well! You can get points by helping other residents and making sure you're polite and follow all the rules. Participate in class and always clean up after yourself in the cafeteria, and be sure to play nice with the other boys!" the woman stood up. She was done. She fidgeted with her bracelet until the colors on it changed and the door behind her opened.

"…and girls." Shawn said, again without really thinking. He was considering what Shakeem had said about getting out, and how many points Shakeem seemed to have in commissary. All he had to do to contact his mom was follow the rules and he could get enough points to write to her maybe. He had tried to swallow these feelings in pranks and manipulating his peers, but maybe it *was* time to just get serious. He lost.

He got caught. Just follow the rules, and get out. Maybe he was just wasting his time here.

"Girls? There haven't been any girls assigned to Paris, no way! That would be a travesty." The woman turned stepped toward the door. "Well! It was nice to meet you! I will see you next week." Shawn was still in thought, not quite listening to the woman anymore, but nodded. "Buh Bye!", she stepped through the door and was gone. The door closed, and Shawn sat in the room alone.

Shawn wondered if he should just tell Frank it's pointless and give it all up. Tell Shakeem he's sorry, and just do whatever Shakeem does; follow the rules, get commissary points, be comfortable, and go home. But maybe… Wait, he thought, did she say girls weren't allowed in Paris? Shawn stood up and looked at the door that was securely closed. He had many, many more questions now, but mainly: what the hell was Ally doing here?

While the other residents played basketball Shakeem and Ally walked together around the outside perimeter of the gymnasium. They reminisced and Shakeem tried to talk about their parents.

"I barely realized you could drive cars manually anymore. I thought all of them were automatic only."

"Yeah, there are still some that have manual features. I think most even have a manual parking feature. You have to always park yourself. But those were phased out, probably before you were even born."

"I think I just wanted to tell myself that something was always off about their death. I wanted to believe it was a malfunction or something."

"I think the biggest malfunction was just that our lives got a lot harder. I was going to go to college you know?"

"Yeah, you wanted to get into an art school, right?"

"Right. I was going to do impressionist paintings, most people do structural designs and things, it just pays more I believe. But those portraits are always formatted to be laser printed into blueprints or something. I wanted to create something that is uniquely human, and uniquely from the soul."

"From the soul that can't be replicated… that can't just be put into a copier and have the same effect."

"Yeah… like I shouldn't be able to put my heart into a brush stroke, or a figure I care about and then have it be copied and mass produced, and still give the same effect to another person afterward. It seems…."

"Cheap. It seems like it's just another mass-produced picture, rather than a work of true art that came from a soul."

"And if it's just able to be produced over and over without a decrease in quality, then what does that say about the artist?"

"Probably that I didn't do a good enough job at putting my soul into the work. That it's hollow and flat... that it's…"

"So basic it's repeatable, constructed, rather than born."

"That sounds awful."

"It does. But art… good art, ensures that the feelings are conveyed regardless."

“I agree.”

They chatted with each other over the period of recreation, and had to part ways soon afterward. Ally was heading to dinner while Shakeem had free time on the cluster. He overheard Shawn and Frank discussing.

“I’m telling you, she said that no girls were supposed to be admitted to Paris. Either she’s not a girl, or this is a big mistake man.” Shawn said in a loud whisper.

“Well, maybe your treatment specialist just didn’t know about the new change? Maybe it’s a brand-new program or some shit.” Frank said in response. Shakeem made his way over to them and made a face that insisted they explain what they were talking about. Shawn shrugged slowly and said, “Well, today I had my first meeting with my treatment specialist, and at the end of the meeting she said there were no girls admitted to Paris. She didn’t say it like there were no programs or anything for girls, like, it was a possibility, she made it sound like it was never going to happen, as if it was an impossibility.” Shawn looked at Shakeem, and then back down to the ground. They all knew that Ally was here to basically get Shakeem out. If Ally was here for what she said first, the computer knew she was a saboteur and put her in here on purpose, then there were little chance things could change. People knew about it, and she was here for good. If, however, it was just a mistake, then maybe when people found out, there would be some hope. Maybe there was a way out. Shakeem wanted more information,

“So you’re saying your treatment specialist didn’t know she was here, and didn’t think it was possible. So that means if you told her again, she would know there was something wrong, right?”

“Well… yeah.. In theory,” Shawn murmured, “But I mean I already told her, and she just brushed over it, like she didn’t really hear me.”

“Yeah, my old T.S. was like that too. Very annoying. But still, if you could make it a point to tell her again, I’d be thankful.” Shakeem turned to Frank and the other boys that were partially listening, “You too, all of you. If you meet with your T.S., let them know that Ally is in here, maybe that’ll help.”

Frank looked around at the faces of the boys, and then back to Shakeem. “Look, we’d like to help and all, but we only get a short time with our treatment specialists as it is. We don’t really get too much time to get caught up on family, and our sentences and stuff. I don’t mind bringing it up or anything…” he looked back at the other boys, then back to Shakeem again, “But I don’t want to waste my time either.” The other boys seemed to agree with Frank’s sentiment. Shawn also realized what it could mean to try to convince his T.S. about Ally. Even if she did believe him, that would mean spending all his time during the session answering questions about Ally. That’s time he could be using to get updates on his own status, or his own behavior. He could see why that time is precious to a lot of the other residents. A few words, sure, just out of respect, but what if she did belong here? Then it’s just a waste of time to bring up the topic entirely.

“Just… Do what you can, okay? I wasn’t asking you to completely abandon your own session, just at the end, or something, mention that you didn’t think women were allowed in the school, and tell the T.S. her name.

See if you can get any information, okay? That's all I meant." Shakeem said, visibly annoyed with their hesitation.

"Sure Shakeem. We got you." Frank said before he walked off. It was just Shawn and Shakeem now, standing next to each other. They were both quiet for quite some time. Shawn finally broke the silence,

"I thought a treatment specialist was supposed to help you actually change, you know? Like help you think of things differently. Mine just basically said what I already knew."

"What's the point, right?" Shakeem agreed.

"Yeah, Ha, really pointless stuff." Shawn added. "But she did remind me about my mother, and how I really have been fucking things up here. I will admit that."

"Yeah, you have." Shakeem was quiet, and felt Shawn's focus shift. He pointed, "You see Frank over there? Laughing with the other guys?"

Shawn nodded. Shakeem continued, "He's been here so long he's forgotten what his kid looks like."

"He has a kid?" Shawn asked. Shakeem nodded,

"Yeah, and his T.S. won't give him a picture of the kid, or any letters from his family until he goes a month without consequences. To show that he's ready to be rehabilitated, ready to take them seriously." Shakeem said.

"… I didn't know that." Shawn said quietly.

"I meant what I said earlier. New guys like to show up and shake things up. I did the same thing when I first showed up. But this isn't a game, Shawn." They were both quiet for a few moments, then Shakeem continued,

"Everyone here wants to get out. But they aren't going to let you until you're ready to actually change." Shakeem and Shawn saw Frank laugh again and the other boys around him join in on a joke they were making.
"Even the laughter is fake." Shakeem said to himself.
"What do you mean?" Shawn asked.
"Frank, and a lot of the other guys, they seem happy, or that they're making it. But back before you came, I spoke to Frank after his T.S. session. I saw his tears; I could see he was crying during the entire session. It's easier for him to live a fake life here than admit that he has growing up to do, and actually want to be a better person. He's been trying to figure out the connection between the collar and the cameras because he wants to be able to beat up his treatment specialist, and bully him into giving the letters from his family. Frank thinks only one step ahead. And because of that, he's landed himself here, and will stay here, until he grows up a little and starts to think about things more thoroughly.... But then you showed up." Shawn looked down, a bit disappointed, knowing where this conversation was going. Shakeem continued,
"You showed up and validated every dumbass thing he was doing. You didn't tell him that it wasn't fucking lasers controlling his collar, or that he was dumb to get consequences over and over again, extending his time at Paris, and keeping him from his family and kid. You didn't convince him it was a fool's errand to try to out think or be faster than a computer system controlling cameras and shit. You let him believe in this fake world, and allowed him to think you two were friends. You made his entire life worse," Shakeem paused to look at Shawn's face, into his eyes, "Because you *felt* like it." Shakeem shook his head and turned around. He

couldn't look at Frank anymore. He couldn't really think about how many weeks or months or even years Frank might be stuck here for simply listening to Shawn's dumb plans. "I know you're able to just, play nice, and outsmart people, and you'll probably get out when you're supposed to. But not everyone can turn their bad behavior on and off. You're lucky to have that ability, that maturity, but people like me, and others in here, had to learn it. Slowly. Consistently. Painfully. We had to learn that our thoughts and actions were wrong. You setting off people because you got bored, or undoing months or years of therapy by provoking people into physical violence because you want to manipulate people stupider than you is fucking disgusting." Shakeem shook his head, then looked back at Shawn. Shawn had his head down, and was sitting on the arm rest of one of the chairs. Shakeem couldn't tell if he was crying or had his eyes closed. Shawn said, very quietly, "I've got a lot to learn. I guess." Shakeem nodded, and walked away. He wasn't satisfied with Shawn's answer, and he was sure Shawn wasn't done playing around. Hell, it was probably all an act; his head down, pretending to cry, whatever. But Shakeem didn't care. He said what he had to say, and the rest wasn't up to him. He decided to relax until dinner.

Dr. Amir ran the simulation again and again in his office. His own console, hidden within faux wall panels and false cabinet doors allowed him to have a miniature control room in his office if he needed it. He didn't want to drag all of his notes and files around the facility, so he had this unit installed for such an occasion. Now that Bernie was secured, and back in his place, and his shareholders, interest groups, media, and superiors were satisfied, it was time to really consider the consequences of his actions. "Once the system is stable, we can modify elements to control overall instability. One must not act quickly at the sacrifice of accuracy," he said to himself as the computers and monitors warmed up into a hefty blue glow. He opened the monitoring software to check the cameras of the facility. He looked at the biometric scans of the security system for both the surrounding administrative building and the correctional facility in the oversized courtyard. He pulled up the image of 4495 and 3022 and placed them next to each other. He set the camera's follow option to 'roaming' which allowed the picture to change from camera to camera as the targets moved around the facility. "What to do… what to do…" he said aloud to himself as he processed other relevant data. He allowed the computer to self-correct most of the error messages that came up. Many of the messages were in the benign, green category. This meant the system was capable of running itself infinitely, but also might need to be assessed at some point in the future. This could mean there was a spill in the cafeteria, or a specific camera was getting dusty, etc. Clearly a maintenance robot would clean the spill during the next cycle, and a repair robot might replace the camera bulb, or wipe it off depending on how bad the obstruction was. Green errors you could most likely ignore. Yellow errors were riskier. This would be if a maintenance robot was down, or if there was a surge of power in one area versus a lack in another. These were anomalies that could be accounted for, but should be monitored, or at least made known. Power surges to certain parts of the building are a regular occurrence, nothing to be concerned about, really. They can, however, trigger certain fail-safes such as turning off equipment that might be needed in that particular area, however. With a few clicks an operator can turn off unnecessary elements of the facility without thinking, and the problem can correct itself over time, but in a rare case, it could be a problem. Dr. Amir let the computer solves those discrepancies as well with certain precautions and priority declarations. Certain functions will never shut off, even in the event of a catastrophic level 6 meltdown. Security systems, the collars, doors and the subsystems that keep them active are core programs that cannot be edited or changed in certain contexts. Dr. Amir himself would have to approve those changes and it would take a while to decouple the process from the rest of the system. Lastly, there are red errors. These errors the computer does not have an answer for. These errors are usually isolated if possible, and allows the computer to make its best judgement if there are no operators online, and to make a call to one if there is a number on file. Dr. Amir's number was always on file, and Bernie's was on file for when he was working, not while on vacation. In the early days of the program, before Bernie changed the protocol to integrate previous models of troubleshooting into future troubleshooting modalities, Dr. Amir would have to drive back from his home to the facility and spend just a few moments instructing the computer what to do. He would stay, of course, to watch the computer make the corrections and change the files that needed to be altered, and then resume green error stability. Errors were inevitable, Dr. Amir thought to himself, but we can at least put them in their place.

While he shifted through some of the current yellow errors on the console, he reminded himself of why he was doing all this. He thought about his work in college focusing on criminal justice and psychology with a minor in physics. He remembered how much effort it took to finally earn a degree in mechanical engineering while also attending medical school and eventually earning licensure in both fields. The testing process, and working with so many people and machines alike was infuriating at times. Many coworkers consider him their subordinate, telling him that his ideas were too radical, and too extreme to ever be considered possible. He gritted his teeth, needing, of course, human help, and smiled and calmly explained why they were wrong, mathematically. After checking his math, people backed off, let him do his work, but always waited for a crack in his armor, a flaw in his logic. The psychology was clear, and honestly it was obvious to Dr. Amir. The psychological associations agreed wholeheartedly. Some were not a fan of the pain element, some thought it could be traumatizing overtime, and so many different profiles of teenagers and children meant there could be a wavering amount of detail for pain tolerance and pain tolerance within context.

It took Dr. Amir a full three years of pure simulated data to convince the association to begin voluntary trials. It took another five years of voluntary trials to prove the system rehabilitated, and there were minimal negative lasting effects. It took another ten years to create the facility in its current state, and after setback and setback, and oversight on top of oversight, he finally obtained the autonomy to function as he saw fit. He possessed the knowledge to rebuild the facility over again if something were to go catastrophically wrong. He could redesign any aspect of the facility if he felt it was necessary. He didn't want to do that, not without helpful, powerful, and first of all, loyal, programmers to help him weed through the massive amounts of data. Dr. Amir was thankful that Bernard Douglas signed onto the project in its early stages, during the voluntary trials to help perfect the counter balancing software. Bernie could probably handle a bit more pain than Dr. Amir could, and when they tried the system themselves, the tests proved as much. With the same consequence, Dr. Amir fell to the ground while Bernie was able to stay upright and also continue walking. Bernie fed this data into the machine for weight, nervous system responses, and positioning of the nanobots for further study.

Dr. Amir remembered those early days fondly. Bernie was rough around the edges, but neither of them liked being told what to do or how to do it. Bernie followed the overall scheme of what Dr. Amir wished, and Dr. Amir didn't micromanage.

"We need the doors to sync up with the camera system so the security guards don't have to watch two separate screens on intake days." Dr. Amir would state reaching over the control room console to hand Bernie a file.

"Put it on the pile, Doc." Bernie would respond, not looking up and gesturing to a big pile of other work he also planned on doing.

"What are you working on Bernie?" Dr. Amir would ask, inquisitively.

"Timing the cafeteria prompts to the vending machines. I would have been done with that by now, but I got a bunch of fucking reds. The school's power output was way too high with each classroom running at full capacity. We can't track a human teacher in each room, and also their offices." Bernie responded, "We need to cut something here or say goodbye to education."

"We can't cut education. If it's merely a holding cell we won't get the approval of the high council, or the public. Locking up youth for months with no growth opportunities never works. I'll get the educational programming. We can simulate the teaching. We can turn the teacher offices into something else, or board it up entirely." Dr. Amir said. "I think we need another form of human interaction anyway."

Later Dr. Amir formed the treatment specialist position and replaced all other human interaction with automation. After the intake liaison, Dr. Amir didn't want any other outside interaction. It was the only way to ensure full control. It was a bold step to eliminate living teachers for autonomous ones, but teachers tend to show biases as well. Dr. Amir remembered his own schooling. Many teachers felt he was pompous or too focused in the data, and missed the overall point of the lesson. In engineering ethics courses, he waved off the verbal debates as a waste of time. If the data showed there was an increase of efficiency and productivity, then keeping around detractors in the building would be a nuisance. He didn't care about aesthetics; he didn't care about selling product to buyers. He wanted to craft and design and create the things that worked and move onto something else. Some called him robotic in this sense. He wasn't fond of 'teachers' in that way. After medical school and specializing in neuropsychiatry, the chemical makeup of the neural tissue was of extreme interest. He spent many thesis projects working on ways to inject, produce, and replace neural tissue as he saw fit in lab animals, and was renown in the field of neuroscience for creating a semi-working rat brain from nothing more than culture. He was able to create a brain from nothing but progenitor cells in a lab, and replace an organic rat brain with his own design. He demonstrated, through data, at least, that the brain was functioning, the rat was still alive, and could perform basic functions such as eat, sleep, mate, and show signs of aggression when threatened. The rat itself died shortly after the procedure, but not before being hailed as a hallmark achievement in the field of medicine and science overall. After that first experiment the cloning, and growing process, has only gotten faster and more streamlined. Since then, many people have replicated these studies and have been attempting human brain creation under strict federal oversite. The field became too hotly contested over for Dr. Amir's liking. Each lab he worked in was equipped with a federal observation device, whether it be a listening device or a camera, or a hybrid of the two. He didn't enjoy the idea that at any moment his difficult nuanced and fragile work would be accosted by idiots with guns and authority. He was disgusted at the very idea of a law enforcement agent with no degrees in any form of science touching his embryonic cultures, or titrations of neurotransmitters. He could not stand that anymore.

Because of his fame, he was able to be awarded many grants for the sum of billions to work on his next project: human rehabilitation. And with generous support from the psychiatric association, which was already being pressured to deliver more substantial results in the field of medicine and social welfare, the project began.

Dr. Amir sat in his chair, in his office, passively resolving errors thinking about how much it took to get to this position. How difficult and how long the process was. For 35 years he had been preparing for this, for this system to function as well as it did, and to continue to develop for years to come. Dr. Chanel had ideas to broaden the concept to businesses and shopping malls, and had done so in limited capacities. Companies such as NeuroRex loved Dr. Chanel's work and wanted a hefty chunk of her time consulting with them, so she was barely around to work on the Paris system herself. Dr. Amir considered retirement. He considered leaving it and letting younger more gritty people take on his work. His thoughts were scattered. No, he wasn't done yet. No, he didn't want to leave. Dr. Chanel could work with NeuroRex and he would stick with PsyClone as a parent company. He would continue to provide them with neurological pattern data, and they would ensure political and public protection. As long as he didn't do anything stupid, the facility would be in good shape. As long as she was taken care of, there wouldn't be any problems, he thought, as he looked at the camera feed watching 4495 eat dinner.

But, what to do? Clearly, he couldn't have an aging woman living amongst boys forever. It was true that the boys would cycle out, of course, and there would be a new set of young men every few months or so, but even still. What if the boys convinced a treatment specialist about this mistake? What if a treatment specialist failed to report this information to him, and instead went public? What would happen if this information got out this way? Or, if a resident was released and convinced their parents to inquire. Nonsense. This was all conspiracy. No one would believe that Paris was secretly holding a woman in their presence. It would be seen as a young boy fantasy; locked in jail with a woman. Sure, he thought, it might be enough to get a tour from a concerned council member, maybe. But there were many areas within the building that could hide a body, living or dead. Dr. Amir smirked to himself. If he wanted to, he could actually end this right now. As a fun exercise he pulled up her nutritional file and looked at her body weight and her kidney's health. Perfectly healthy, he thought to himself, no abnormalities at all. He looked at her liver. All good, he thought again. He could, over time, increase her nutritional profile and as she selected her food items increase the salt content slowly over time. As she ate, she would get accustomed to the taste, and eventually go into a coma. He could have her dead, or at least gone from view in a matter of months if he wanted it to be a secret. He closed those files. Poisoning seemed to be beneath him. Also, there would be red errors if a resident didn't wake up in the morning without normal prompting and standard consequences.

He watched still. Watched her clean up her area quietly, and alone. He watched the other boys dash to the line ahead of her, and her slowly, gracefully stand on the line at the back. He saw one of the boys in front of her earn a small harmless consequence for turning around to talk to her. She smiled a bit, but said nothing. Annoying, he thought. The notion to kill her seemed so obvious, yet he didn't want to think about it. At this point there clearly was no other option. Maybe if they had more time, and if he had been more aware of what A.I.L. was doing, he could have stopped all this. Perhaps after A.I.L. did this nonsense, he could have let her go, and just trusted she wouldn't have said anything, maybe make a deal or something. Naïve, he thought to himself, you're being naïve. There's no way anyone on that tour wasn't just looking for dirt on his facility. That's what they all wanted. Every single person in that room wanted to see the facility shut down, and each one of them wanted to be the straw that sent it crumbling. If a tour member got mixed into the resident population, there was no doubt the public would hear about it, and no doubt PsyClone would consider Paris a threat to their image as well. They already had issues with protesters clamoring on about clone-rights and other silly ethical issues. They didn't need their new venture to also include public relation scandals and conspiracies.

Dr. Amir shook his head. There was no use. She had to be contained. Damn it A.I.L. If he, or Bernie, just looked up that afternoon, if they just watched the computer a bit longer, they would have seen something go wrong. Dr. Amir sighed. "Well, we're here now. So, what do I do?" He pulled up the collar application and looked at the one dedicated to her. The computer was still confused when detailing the collar for an additional resident. There was a note in the file suggesting that one resident received two collars, A, and B. Resident 3022 seemed to be doing well so far, and his collar seemed to rarely need deactivation anymore. Not only that, but a contingency plan for 3022 was already in place. "He'll be dealt with shortly," he said to himself quietly.

Dr. Amir rarely looked at individual resident files anymore. He used to constantly. To him, they were his lab rats, and he always treated them special. They belonged to him, his test subjects. No undue or unscheduled harm was to come to them. In this setting, he felt the same with his residents, and refused to call them inmates. They resided in his experimental chamber, providing a service to the community, and advancing human control and habitation. Rehabilitation, was just the icing to give those with money a reason to spend. The rest was purely for science.

He toyed with the idea in his mind. He could, perhaps, just lead her to her room and deactivate the collar. The nanobots would swarm, and eventually she would die in agony. Then again, that would be cruel. You never exterminate a lab rat with malice, he remembered, you simply let it fall asleep. He considered just leaving her in her room, and never letting her out again. He could increase the sensitivity of consequences so that if she spoke, she would be given a consequence, and that way she couldn't cry for help or make a ruckus. That would be psychologically cruel, Dr. Amir thought. Then, Dr. Amir thought, there might be a way where everyone gets exactly what they want. Dr. Amir opened up the nanobot configuration page, and started to run a few simulations. "At least this way, it'll be quick." He said.

"Sorry Ally," Eddy said looking up at her at his desk, "No press pass. We've already got a joint agreement with CityNews, and they'll be present in full, so we don't need anyone to go to this." Ally was disappointed.

"Well, don't you want more information on Paris as a whole? This could be lucrative, especially if I go on the tour. I'm sure CityNews wouldn't share everything if there was an exclusive tour inside the facility." Ally tried to make her presence necessary.

"Sorry kid, no one cares about Paris anymore. Back a few years ago when that one kid killed himself, and years before when it was a coed thing, people were sort of invested, but we have other things to worry about. Did you finish that article on the weather satellite blowing up? That was big news." Eddy shuffled some papers and looked off at his computer monitor. Ally stood there, still trying to think of something to convince him. She couldn't think of anything. If no one cared, then even if she did write a story, Eddy wouldn't be able to approve it for publishing anyway. She didn't want to tell him her personal investment, that would throw her credibility away for sure. She wasn't sure what to do, but she did know one other person she could ask.

Ally left the office and went through her contact lists. These were sources for other articles she had written, and other quotes she had gathered. It turns out one of the council men for the city was a previous source that just happened to have the head of the Department of Corrections in his pocket. If she could get a meeting with him, convince him somehow to get a press pass from the DOC, then she could go as a private contractor of the city. She'd report all she could to her office, of course, she was loyal to Eddy, and the DownTown Press. They gave her a job without any experience and barely a functioning resume. Without them, she really wouldn't have been able to survive with her brother alone in the world. She had to go behind their back this time, though. Just this once.

She left a message for the councilman, and laid on the charm as thick as she could. This was the only other way, she told herself. Ally didn't have many friends; she didn't do many social things. Before her parents died, she had friends in school and small circles of people she would hang out with, but her real joy was being with her brother. Many people talked about how much they hated their siblings, or how their younger brother was always in the way or annoying. Ally listened politely, but never felt the same way. Even when her brother was causing trouble, especially after their parents died, she still felt a strange connection to him. In a sense, she felt that he was part of her, an extension of her very being. Sometimes, she noticed, when he felt sad, so did she, and sometimes, in an uncanny sense, she could sense his feelings and thoughts sometimes. It wasn't some magical psychic thing, it was just a strong intuition she had when he was in trouble, or having extreme thoughts, she figured. She would leave her afterschool classes and rush home to do homework with him one afternoon, to instead find law enforcement officers, a therapist, and of course, her brother standing by the front door. There was an accident. Both dead. Ally looked at her brother as the words of the officers and the therapist started to fade away. She looked at her brother and just saw his blank and empty expression. The happy boy she wanted to study with was gone. A light went out behind his eyes and left a darkened room full of pain.

After that he stopped talking much. They lived together in the house for a while with a social worker checking in on them week to week. They were wards of the state, but considered autonomous entities. Because Ally was soon to be a legal adult, and showed maturity, she was given custody of her brother and could live where they wished. With the insurance money and some other charities, they would be okay until Ally finished school and found a good job; then he started getting into trouble.

Her brother would wind up breaking something, or hitting someone. A fine for this broken window, a citation for this misdemeanor, one week in juvie for hitting a teacher, another fine for vandalism. Paying for a lawyer for just one offense was hard enough, and the days just became harder. Despite all of this, Ally graduated, and they had a nice celebration day together. She remembered that they ordered the same ice cream cone, and she tried not to get any on her cap and gown. They laughed together when she inevitably spilled some on herself, and ruined the gown before the day was out. The day ended as any: sitting on the couch in their apartment, laying on each other as the glow of the TV highlighted the faces of two smiling teenagers, alone in the world, but together.

"Fucking…" he wheezed, "mother…" another wheeze, "fucker…", wheeze. Bernie looked at the new security protocols in place. He also looked at the nanobot configuration Dr. Amir had created. He pounded on his desk in rage. "You Mother Fucker!" He growled, and wheezed afterward. Bernie had not been permitted to leave. Bernie didn't necessarily ask either, but he was too proud to beg to be let out of his cage. Bernie did his work; it was <u>his</u> work after all. He designed the system that gave him this job, and he decided how to make the job obsolete after time. It was, in all senses, his work. But in addition to this, he made sure to follow all the changes Dr. Amir had put in place as well. He kept track of the old system files and where Dr. Amir put them, and made copies of everything. He was running out of space, however; this system wasn't as fortified as the control room, but what he didn't copy, he memorized and wrote down the gist of so he could replicate them if needed. He tried his best to maintain the changes and guess what the reasons were for. In this particular case, he saw the nanobot reconfiguration of 4495 and saw exactly what it was for.

"He's going to fucking kill that poor girl…" he stated to himself, looking at the new task of the bots. "They're going to funnel into her heart and then rip it apart, that bastard." Bernie wheezed and looked around the room. There was nothing. He thought about heroically bashing the two guards outside the door with a computer monitor or something, but recognized immediately that he would be shot. Bernie went back over to his files. Maybe, Bernie considered, he could write a covert file under a basic error fix, a virus, maybe, that just cancels the new configurations. No, no, he reconsidered, the virus protection makes all covert files plain, and Dr. Amir would know to thoroughly check everything from Bernie now on. Damn it. What could he do?

Before he could think of a solution, he saw another file flagged. 4495's disposition order was being rewritten to release. Along with other changes to the file and the systems underneath, her time was being changed to 0 days left to serve. Dr. Amir was about to release her. Bernie was confused. Why would he release her now? Didn't he want to kill her and hide the body? He stopped fussing around in his chair. He looked around the room and felt a deep sense of loss. "I… really… can't do anything." He wheezed quietly and leaned back in his chair. "Fuck."

It was the middle of the night when the localized speaker in Ally's room lit up. "Ms. Aliyah Shakeem, there has been a misunderstanding. Please report to the Intake door for your release." The door slid open, and a green line along the floor lit up, along with her collar. Ally barely had her eyes open. "W-what?" Ally said sitting up sluggishly. The speaker repeated the message, "Ms. Aliyah Shakeem, there has been a misunderstanding. Please report to the Intake door for your release." Aliyah stood up and rubbed her eyes. "What...release? Really?" She started to sober up. This… this is great, she thought. It was just a mistake. Last names were the same, computer malfunction. Great! She would be out soon and could continue her work. She stood up and walked out onto the green line. She followed it onto the cluster. Everyone was asleep at the moment, and the massive room was completely silent. Nothing was moving, and some of the main lights were even off. Ally felt a spookiness about the place, as if the entire building was deserted. She felt as if she alone was left. The last survivor. She followed the line out of habit then stopped in her tracks. What about her brother? She paused for a moment and considered returning to her room. She forced herself to continue. "No, I already screwed up by getting myself stuck in here, I won't ruin a chance to leave." She told herself. She continued to walk; it would be easier to negotiate after she was let out of there. If she was on the outside, she could talk to people about these new developments. Now that they had really fucked up by trapping her in there, she had some room for negotiations. She had some power now; she could make demands. Ally smiled to herself as she walked. She did it. She would leave the facility, talk to Dr. Amir, or someone high up and demand her brother's release or else she would tell the press. After her brother was safe, she might move somewhere far away, and release a story anyway. Eddy said no one cared about Paris, sure, but if their own reporter was kidnapped and held in prison for weeks, clearly there would be a story worth printing. These people thought they were doing things for the greater good, when they were just torturing teenagers for being teenagers. Sure, some of them deserved rehabilitation, and some even punishment. But at the heart of it all, they were just boys. They needed to be taught and listened to, not attacked from the inside out.

Ally made it to the intake door, and it opened in a hiss. She stepped into the room she saw just a week or two ago, and continued into the hallways that led to the outside administration office. Dr. Amir was waiting by the door.

"Ms. Shakeem, I'm so glad to see you unharmed. We must apologize for the mix up."

"I, I hope you know I am very disappointed by the unprofessional nature of this entire facility." Ally responded, finding her adult words again. After talking to teenage boys, she had to quickly code switch. Boys were direct, adults spoke in puzzles.

"I'm terribly sorry, and I take personal responsibility. When our security system tested your blood, it confused you with another resident, and caused quite a bit of confusion. We have been working on your release for quite some time." Dr. Amir apologized once more.

"*Weeks*? It took *weeks* to open the door?" Aliyah spoke sternly at him, not letting up.

Dr. Amir bowed his head to show his compliance, “The system is very complex, and this *is* a detention facility, no doors are merely opened at Paris, Ms. Shakeem. Once our programmers were clear what to do and able to perform the actions, we did what we could to ensure the release of you, and the protection of the other residents simultaneously.”

“I just need to get out of here.” Aliyah said, stepping forward, “Get this awful collar off of me.”

“Yes. This is also a tricky thing. I can remove the collar for you, but first I’ll have to break the seal and unlock the mechanism. The only tool we have to do that is in the surgery room. Please follow me.” Dr. Amir turned to walk forward, and Ally followed, much like during the tour.

As they entered the surgery room, Ally felt her anxiety grow. There was a vagueness around this entire situation that made her feel as if she was dreaming. A passing clock read 1:00 AM, and it felt similarly but the facility seemed too empty to be real. It was just her own footsteps echoing back at her on the marble floors, and Dr. Amir seemed too confident in simply letting her leave. Shouldn’t he be asking for her to keep this quiet, or at least trying to pay her off?

Dr. Amir asked her to lay down on one of the operating tables. She did so. Dr. Amir took a rectangular device with a sharp needle-like appendage extending from one side and stood over Ally’s body. Ally lay there, wondering if this was yet another trick she had fallen for. She blindly trusted A.I.L. and got herself stuck in the facility, should she blindly trust Dr. Amir, who says she can leave? What real reason would there be to lie, after all? He couldn’t explain why there was a grown woman in a juvenile facility for boys, right? He had to let her go, there was no other option. Her thoughts were interrupted,

“This…” Dr. Amir said, while still looking at the device’s screen, “…will target the nanobots in your system, and deactivate them. Then we can turn off the necklace and remove it.”

“Collar.” Ally corrected him.

“Collar…?” Dr. Amir asked.

“It’s a collar, not a necklace.” Ally stated again. She had to wear one of these damn things, she was going to be the one to make sure he called it what it was.

“Collar, then.” Dr. Amir stated, sensing this distinction was important for her, for some reason.

Ally looked at the ceiling. It was quiet again as Dr. Amir pressed buttons and typed figures into the device. Ally began to hear the buzz and whirr of other machinery in the room. “What surgery do the inmates receive?” Ally asked.

“Is this off the record, Ms. Shakeem?” Dr. Amir asked. He was going to answer either way, he just always wanted to say that.

“No, none of this is off the record. Why should it be?” Ally asked, feeling her hidden anger begin to show up.

“I didn’t mean it that way,” Dr. Amir retreated, “I just wanted to know if what you’re asking is from a place of curiosity, or journalistic professionalism. It modifies the answer slightly.”

“Why would it matter? Does the public have the right to know?” Ally asked.

"Of course, and officially speaking, Paris is open to inquiry, and even the occasional tour, of course. But the inner workings of the facility aren't usually too interesting, you see. Results are all I hear about in meetings. Results, figures and statistics. Those are the things people care about, usually. So, if someone asks me something more technical, I get ahead of myself. I apologize." Dr. Amir paused. Ally said nothing.

"The surgery is for whatever the resident needs before entering. Some of these boys come in with broken teeth if they were in a fight, some with infected tonsils, many with appendixes that may rupture during their stay. We take care of all of those things before they're admitted so there is no need for an emergency trip to the hospital. Also, it's on the city's dime, so the resident doesn't have to pay the bill after they leave, or anything." Dr. Amir continued talking, "I know a lot of people see this place as monstrous, and the mystery within it is tantalizing, but when you do get a chance to look at it all, it's just a normal facility. The neckla—the collars, are of course hotly contested, and the nanobot consequences are painful,"

"You're telling me?" Ally interrupted.

"… But for those who really did not have discipline growing up, or have failed to learn how a society works, these self-contained consequences are important. It's how our brains learn right from wrong, and how we grow as people. There. Done."

There was a little click, and a cracking noise as Dr. Amir put down his device on a nearby counter, and removed the collar from around Ally's neck. Ally rubbed her neck with her hands and scratched a sore spot. She sat up and slid off the table. Dr. Amir took the collar and placed it on the counter next to the device. He handed Ally a new shirt and pants, and turned around while she changed, leaving the Paris issued clothes on the operating table. "I hope you write a well written article, and I hope to see it before you publish, just so I know what sort of thing I'm dealing with, Ms. Shakeem."

Ally frowned, "I'm going to be honest with the world. They'll see what happens here."

"I'm just glad it was you and no one else that got trapped here. How is your brother, by the way?" Dr. Amir stated. Ally stopped talking and stared, it was puzzle time. "It was quite clear that you and a resident shared the same DNA, it's the only way you could be confused with a resident. While it was a fluke, and the problem has since been corrected, it's clear that your bias against this organization is due to your next of kin being incarcerated here." Dr. Amir said, "In other words, write whatever you want, and we will too."

"Are you threatening to discredit me?" Ally asked, taking a step forward, "I will not be bullied into submission by anyone, you hear me? Your facility captured and imprisoned a law-abiding citizen. There is no way around that. And there is no way you can claim bias on such a fact. This place records everything, I've seen the fucking cameras, you can't hide that I was here, and you can't hide all the fucking data that goes through this place. I was here, against my will, and against all authority. How dare you pretend that there is an inkling of self-preservation here. This is disgusting. I'm out of here." Ally turned in a rage and stomped off toward the door.

"Like I said, I look forward to reading it." Dr. Amir stated and followed, at a distance, as Ally found the exit. The security officers looked a bit stunned as she appeared first on their monitors, and then in front of them. Dr. Amir waved his hand, signaling to open the doors. They did so, and Ally said nothing. She continued to storm out of the doors into the next checkpoint. Dr. Amir told the guards to make sure she left, and to give her an auto-ride to her apartment. The security guard told Dr. Amir that the shipment had arrived. He told them to bring it in after their guest had left.

Ally barely said anything as she stormed off into the parking lot. Her anger was fueled by the need to prove this bastard wrong. She would burn the entire building down if she had to, but people were going to listen. They had to listen. Ally's auto-ride was parked next to a PsyClone truck, and the security guard opened the door for her. She sat in the auto-ride, a very nice model, she noted, and started to draft the article in her head as the vehicle began to move. She thought about her stay, and which parts were the most insane. "Walking in a line, like robots!" she said out loud, but then thought about it. Besides breaking the rules, what part of the facility was inhumane? "The lack of human connection! Of course!" she said, again, to no one but herself as the auto-ride found its way to the main road. But her memory was filled with being able to talk to her brother without issues, extensive free time and recreational time, not to mention cafeteria time. In fact, the only time she was truly alone was in her room for bed time, and she preferred it that way. She tried to find a way to spin the article to make the facility look horrendous, but she couldn't deny that the programs themselves were not at fault. She started to feel her throat fill up, and her eyes began to get moist. "They'll just see it as a mix up, a tabloid piece. 'Random reporter says she was locked up unfairly!' who really cares? There wasn't anything wrong with that place. I just shouldn't have been there." Ally cried, feeling that this entire endeavor was a waste. "and… I… I didn't even get to say good bye." This made her sob, as she remembered looking at her brother one last time.

The auto-ride stopped and Ally got out. She made her way to the lobby and used her name and code to get the spare key. She went up to her apartment which was as she left it. No one had claimed it yet. She ignored the living room couch and went to sit on her bed, the bottom bunk, and continued to cry. She was right back where she started. Everything she did, every lead she followed, every moment trying to work for an extra dollar to afford a lawyer and sue Paris for keeping her brother locked up for so long. Every single time she turned down dates, or company parties, or even just a lazy Saturday morning because she had to work, or sleuth, or write, or interview someone, all for her to end up on her bed, in her crappy apartment, alone.

She felt her heart grow heavy. She clutched her chest as she cried. "It.. it hurts.. it hurts", she whimpered to herself, tears down her face and saliva bubbling up in her mouth. "my.. my heart is on fire", she cried as she squeezed her chest harder. Her heart started to bleed as the nanobots were released from their dormancy timer and began ripping her heart apart from the inside, a souvenir from Paris. Aaliyah laid there, struggling to speak and unable to move as she felt her body quickly shut down. She hyperventilated as she became dizzy, and slowly, her crying turned to gurgling then into silence.

Eddy received Ally's resignation over e-mail and sighed. He was working late, way later than he usually did, and was still at his office. He didn't want to lose a good worker, but that's what happens when you hire young go-getters. They're always off on the next big thing. He silently wished her luck on her future endeavors, and then focused on his monitor, that had the latest story about a new rocket launch toward the Martian colony.

Shakeem lay in bed awake. He couldn't sleep. He stared at the ceiling of his cell, and felt a twinge of sadness. He was sad that his sister was here, and not out in the world somewhere, doing something great with her life. He felt his heart flutter for some reason, and sat up. The muted glow from the camera eye near the speaker stayed dim. He laid back down, not sure what that feeling was for, but he didn't like it. He felt uneasy, and partially nauseous. He tried to go back to sleep, when the light turned from dim to bright.

Bernie was overwhelmed with what was going on. He could only watch data deletions and file transfers. He was unable to reach the outside world, and he was unable to do anything from the inside. All he could do was watch. Resident 3022 was modified to return back to release on time, tomorrow even. Bernie was confused to see a new PsyClone entry file on 3022 that was already redacted, but clearly brand new. The files were sealed and Bernie didn't have access to it. "Figures," he wheezed, "fucking figures." He continued to watch over the few hours as 4495's file was deleted without a trace. No intake. No disposition. No nutrition file, no medical files, no releases, nothing. 4495 merely disappeared. Bernie was in denial at first, and remembered his personal files he still had. He wondered if Dr. Amir was smart enough to search his stuff at his home, or to wipe the files in the control room backup drives. "Intellectual bastard, probably did it already. Fuck!" Bernie yelled again to himself, while stuck in his office. "God Damn it."

Later that night while Bernie was monitoring the maintenance robots, he noticed a lit-up line on the ground. He looked at the stream of data and wondered if it was a malfunction. However, no, there were no errors. To his surprise he saw a very sleepy looking resident, one Bernie recognized as 3022, J. Shakeem, wandered out into the hallway following the line toward the intake. Bernie couldn't quickly switch his views as easily as he used to, and before he could switch to see the intake pavilion's cameras, 3022 seemed to disappear into the intake door. He blinked to himself, wondering if he was just sleep deprived, but clearly he saw the resident walk down the hallway and enter the room, yet while looking in the room he clearly entered, there was nothing. He refreshed the feed multiple times; maybe there was a bug or a glitch. Nothing was showing up. Everything was quiet.

Bernie figured he had made a mistake, and he couldn't access the recordings without requesting specific feeds from Dr. Amir, who probably wasn't even in the facility at the moment. He decided to continue watching the maintenance of a certain loose tile in the hallway, and then he saw it again. It looked like, after close inspection, the same resident from behind, walking toward the cluster doors, following a guideline. The only difference was that his gait seemed stiffer, less confident. "The fuck is this?!" Bernie yelled to himself, loud enough that the guards outside his door could hear.

“Quiet in there!” One guard said,
“Blow it out your ass, you fucker!” Bernie responded, while still looking at the screen, he switched feeds to the cluster, and saw nothing once more. This was impossible. He queried the system once more for any changes to the security camera footage, and saw nothing. He looked again through the system for any leaks or errors. He even combed through the green level errors to make sure he didn’t miss anything. But there was nothing. He finally decided to write a message to Dr. Amir. He explained the phenomenon, and the times he saw the feed and asked for an explanation. After he sent the message, he continued to watch the feed, expecting to receive an answer some time later the next day. To his surprise, he received one immediately.

“I’m sorry you saw that, Bernard, if you’re on a camera feed live, it seems like I can’t disable it remotely. However, it’s in your best interest to forget you saw that. Goodnight.”

Dr. Amir’s response just made Bernie angrier. This is fucking nuts, Bernie thought. This fucker is insane, he said to himself. Bernie stood up and paced around his cage, his cell. He couldn’t do anything, he concluded. He couldn’t do anything but keep all the live feeds open that he could. He’d be able to see everything as it happened, at least, he thought. If he couldn’t do anything, he could at least just watch everything. He sighed, and took out another notebook. He wrote down what he saw along with the date and time. That’s all he could do.

Shakeem woke up and looked at the camera to complete eye contact. He heard the prompts from the ceiling and his localized speaker, and followed the line along with his peers to the hygiene stations. He bathed, as always, and put on his clothes, as always, and waited for the schedule of the day. Today was the day. While it typically would have been an enjoyable time, he was a bit annoyed, more so than usual, because of so many jokes the other guys played on him. He kept to himself and left well enough alone, but for some reason the other guys continued to poke fun. He was about to be released, and sure, some guys took that hard. They overall liked it when one of their boys left, but they also had to throw some jokes his way too. Shakeem understood it, but he still didn't like it.

"Hey man, where's that sister of yours?", one would say at lunch.

"Yeah, man, she was going to help me with my math, what gives?" another might ask.

"Sarcastic assholes," Shakeem would think, not giving them the satisfaction of an answer.

"She was here a few days ago, man, what happened? Was she released?" another boy asked.

"Are you done?" Shakeem would eventually respond sarcastically, and move to another table. He was tired of it. He missed his sister more than anything, and he couldn't wait to see her again. All the guys acting like they knew her or something was just annoying him. No one knew her, no one knew her like he did.

Shakeem met up with Shawn and Frank at recreation, and played table tennis. They were in teams with another resident, and played a few games. Shawn finally asked, "So, she's really gone then, huh?"

"Ah, you too huh? We were getting along, why are you doing this too?" Shakeem asked.

"Wh-What do you mean? We all respected her, you know?" Shawn responded. "Would've been nice to say goodbye is all."

"Yeah, she was a nice person. We all saw how much you two cared about each other" Frank chimed in.

"Are we playing or not?" the other resident asked.

"Stop acting like you all knew her, alright. It's getting old. I know it's a prank or whatever, but just fucking cut it out" Shakeem growled as he served the ball to Frank and his teammate.

"I mean, we didn't know her extensively, or anything. But for the short time she was here, it was nice, you know?" Shawn continued. Shakeem slammed the paddle down, missing the ball as it came to him.

"Ha ha! We win again!" the other resident said

"Just, fucking cut it out. You've never even seen my sister before. Just stop it." Shakeem said, loud enough for the entire gymnasium to hear.

"What are you talking about Shakeem? Ally was here for like weeks." Shawn said,

"Yeah, I mean, we're sad she left, but anyone getting out of here is a good day, know what I mean?" Frank joined in.

"She was hot too, not gunna lie," the other resident added.

"Fuck you guys. I don't mind taking an extension if it means shutting you all up." Shakeem vaguely threatened and walked off to the bleachers.

“What’s wrong with him?” Frank asked Shawn.
“I don’t know, maybe he’s in denial or something?” Shawn replied, “He’s pretending she wasn’t ever here for some reason. Maybe it’s easier for him somehow.”
“Woo! And she had a nice ass,” the other resident said, missing the tone of the conversation, “Are we playing again?” he asked, serving the ball to Shawn.

Shakeem was later moved to the intake room for release. He was given a copy of his disposition orders to reflect the full time of his stay, a transcript of his studies while he was at the facility to be transferred as credits for any school he chose, a particular amount of money so he could at least find transportation, new clothes, and food, along with the address of the employment office. He was wished good luck, and after his final assessment from a psychologist, he was free to go. “Good bye James” the doctor said.

James was dropped off at his sister’s apartment and found his way up to their door. He knocked to find that the place was no longer owned by her. He went back down to the lobby to do a search for her name.

Deceased.

The last patron was deceased, by this lobby's computer. James didn't feel right. His brain wasn't quite understanding what was going on. This wasn't possible. He left the lobby and found a public telephone nearby. He called her number to no avail. Disconnected. He thought it was odd that the Paris liaison didn't name anyone next of kin, but he figured it didn't matter, some clerical error. He walked to a public transport and used some money to get a ride to the Hall of Records. He quietly entered and did an inquiry of Aliyah Shakeem. Again, deceased.

He felt his heart ache and a hollow feeling grew in his chest. His brain started to go blank once more as he failed to make sense of what he read. He forced himself to read the entry.

"Aaliyah Shakeem, is survived by her younger brother, James Shakeem (Last location known: PYCF). Aaliyah was found in her apartment after an apparent heart attack. She was a reporter for the DownTown Press and had positive relationships with her employer. Aaliyah did jobs around town to get by, and was a positive element of the city."

James read the details; the dates, the times, and the autopsy report, through wet eyes, and quickly wiped away his tears. He sat on that stool and cried quietly to himself for a while. He had nothing now.

He was nothing without her.

James found himself sitting in the employment office. With the credits from Paris, he was considered a graduate of high school and could be qualified for human-relation jobs. He was called into a small office and was asked the basic questions about likes, dislikes, history, etc.

"… I just got out of Paris Correctional, so I don't have a lot of experience" James explained.

"Oh, very good. Many places like to see that. Paris, wow! It means you have mastered discipline." The clerk said as he wrote down those details on his computer screen, he didn't notice James' slight grimace at that statement. "Well, it seems like there are a few entry jobs here. Looks like DownTown Press is looking for an intern…. ah and PsyClone is looking for intermediate test subjects, oh, and there is a local grocer that needs help as well. They all pay pretty well, but they're all fairly temporary."

"I'll try the grocery; it seems like simple work. Maybe I'll try art in my down time." James said after some thought.

"Oh! You're an artist?" The clerk responded, clicking and clacking away on the keyboard.

"No. My sister always wanted to be one."

"Ah, you want to complete her dreams for her hm?" The clerk said, only partially listening.

"In a way, I hope to be just like her." James said, mostly to himself.

Attachments II

DATE: <Redacted>

TIME: <Redacted>

PSYClone Industries Office <REDACTED> Transcribed Meeting Note

DNA Sequence of J. Shakeem, Age 16 Transcribed and Duplicated into new host in entirety. DNA Sequence uploaded with neural inputs from Paris Files 3022.

New Host (J. Shakeem) will be synthesized in 2 weeks.

Reason listed: <REDACTED>

DATE: <Redacted>

TIME: <Redacted>

PSYClone Industries Office <REDACTED> Transcribed Meeting Note

DNA sequence duplicated successfully, new host growth to potential (age 16) and ready to be extracted from final enclosure. J. Shakeem will be delivered to Paris Youth Correctional Facility for internal processing.

DNA sequence 660432261G22 Host

DNA sequence 660432261G22 Clone (100% duplicated)

NeuroRex Enterprise

"A soul dances with the soulless and the void between them births life."

Bernard Douglas

"Treasure that which cannot be replicated."

Eddy, the Editor

"God bless all forms of life, from all points of origin."

PsyClone Industries

"Put the power of creation in the hands of the created."

Epilogue

Shawn sat down at the desk and waited. The door opened up and his treatment specialist sat down in a huff, placing all her files and papers in a scattered pattern on the desk. She looked up at Shawn and smiled, as if she had just accomplished some meaningful task. "Phew!", she said in an exaggerated tone.

"I have to tell you something." Shawn said. The treatment specialist smiled and looked extremely pleased.

"Oh? That's wonderful! The relationship between treatment specialist and resident is one of the most important elements to rehabilitation. My last resident didn't seem to care much for me…" She went on.

Shawn interrupted, "Look, -- uh," He stopped, "…what is your name anyway?"

"Oh! I forgot to tell you!? I'm so so so sorry! My name is Karah, and I'll be your treatment specialist!" Karah said, as if the greeting was memorized. Nothing about her was sincere, Shawn thought.

"Well, about what I want to tell you…" Shawn looked away, "No… Never mind, you wouldn't be interested…"

"Shawn. You can tell me anything, and I'll believe you, of course!" Karah said.

"I…. well… It's about… No, never mind. Let's just stay on script." Shawn said, pretending to be unable to continue.

"Shawn, talk to me, no matter how outlandish or crazy it might be I'll listen to you!"

Shawn looked back at her, and then down again, and let out a big sigh, "You're not going to believe me." Shawn said, eventually.

"Please, Shawn." Karah said.
"Well, it's about this other resident I knew… his sister really… Ah, no it's stupid. Forget it." Shawn said, pretending to look away again.
"Shawn, it's okay… look," Kara fidgeted with the buttons on her wrist. The lights dimmed slightly. There was a whirr in the room and the speaker announced, "Camera Deactivated". Karah smiled at Shawn. "There, now. What is going on?"

Shawn looked down, to conceal his smirk.

About the Author

Robert L. Hawkins III, MS, is a mental health therapist in Philadelphia, PA. He holds degrees in Neuroscience and Clinical Mental Health Counseling. Mr. Hawkins draws on his education and experience to create a futuristic, dystopian world where juvenile discipline, science and technology intersect. *Corrected* is heralded for its compelling characters, its weaving together of multiple writing styles and genres, and its vividly creative storyline. This is the first in a series of fictional works soon to be released by this talented writer.

www.ingramcontent.com/pod-product-compliance
Lightning Source LLC
LaVergne TN
LVHW041925090826
845145LV00015B/693

* 9 7 8 0 9 8 4 9 4 7 7 3 7 *